Frozen

Michael Smith

Dedication

This book is dedicated to my mother, **Shirley Smith**, who always told me, *"There isn't anything in this world you can't do. You can be anything you want if you work hard and try."*
Mom, you were my biggest cheerleader, and your belief in me has guided my every step.

I also dedicate this book to my father, **Milton Morrison**, who helped me navigate the big city of Los Angeles. Your wisdom, encouragement, and constant support kept me grounded. *Thanks, Pop.*

And last, but certainly not least, to my beautiful wife, **Kim**, the moment I saw you walking across our college campus 44 years ago, I knew you would forever be my love and my greatest support.

To my two amazing daughters, **Shannon** and **Sydney**, you both will face challenges and moments of adversity in life. Through it all, keep your faith in God, stay strong, and remember that with faith and perseverance, you can accomplish anything you set your hearts on.

Acknowledgment

I would like to acknowledge the many friends, relatives, and brothers, past and present, whose advice and encouragement inspired me to write this book.

Mark Parham first encouraged me years ago, back in Atlanta, to write a book, and his words have stayed with me ever since.

To my cousin, **John "Butch" Patterson**, a lobbyist for the Ohio Hospital Association, thank you for being such a strong influence in my life growing up. *Rest in peace, Butch.*

To **Kwame Barnett**, who started an organization in college that helped connect me with my brothers, a bond that continues even today, thank you for your leadership and friendship.

To **Jay Jackson**, who played semi-pro baseball and was loved by the kids at the Boys & Girls Club, your words, *"Michael, step up to the plate and take your cuts,"* will always stay with me. *Rest in peace, J-Dawg.*

To **Andre Dawson**, my fraternity brother, investigator, and detective with the Los Angeles Police Department, I miss you dearly. *Love you, Duke.*

To **Lawrence Claxton**, my track brother who was recruited with me at Western Michigan, *rest in peace, my brother.*

Special thanks to **Lee Bailey**, **Rayford Frye**, and **Dennis Jones**, who supported my wife Kim in organizing a GoFundMe page when I had my stroke, your kindness will never be forgotten.

To **Robert Janisse**, who gave me my first opportunity in the pharmaceutical industry, and **Andy Corley**, who believed in me and offered me a chance to work with a start-up company, thank you both for opening doors and for your trust.

All of you have made a lasting difference in my life, thank you from the bottom of my heart.

And finally, a special thanks to **Leah David** and her amazing team at **Book Writing Maestros** for helping bring this vision to life.

About the Author

Michael Smith, originally from Yellow Springs, Ohio, is a proud graduate of Western Michigan University. He was recruited to Western on a full athletic scholarship for track and field, where he became a Mid-American Conference Champion and earned his degree in Communications within four years.

In 1981, Michael moved to Los Angeles, California, where he began a successful career in pharmaceutical and medical device sales. Despite having no prior experience in the field, his determination and work ethic propelled him to the top, earning numerous honors and recognition as one of the leading sales executives in the nation across several organizations.

Michael wrote this book to **inspire and motivate young people**, showing them that there is nothing in this world they cannot achieve. His message is clear: **have a dream, stay driven, and never give up on success.**

Table of Contents

Chapter 1:
Where It All Began

I was born in Springfield, Ohio, a place that left its fingerprints on everything I became. I don't remember the hospital, the room, or the weather that day. What I do remember is the small room where my mom and I lived. It was upstairs, in the back of a house. Just one room for both of us. That was home.

My bed sat on one side. My mom's was on the other. There was just enough space between for us to move around. It wasn't fancy or big, but it was ours. It smelled like old wood and clean laundry, with just a faint hint of whatever was cooking across the street at the meat market. That's right—there was a meat market right across from us, just off Center Street. I can still hear the creaky back steps that led up to our place. We never used the front. The rear staircase was how we came and went every day.

Those stairs weren't just a way in and out—they were part of my story. I remember one day, helping Mom carry groceries. I had a bag in one hand and a glass bottle of milk in the other. I was trying to be helpful, trying to be grown. I lost my grip halfway up and the bottle slipped. It shattered on the steps. As I tried to pick up the pieces, one sharp edge caught my wrist. Blood poured down my arm. It wasn't a deep cut, but deep enough that Mom took me to get stitches. I still have the scar. When I look at it now, it reminds me of those early days. It's just a little line, but it carries so much memory.

Our routine was like clockwork. Most mornings, before the sun even thought about rising, Mom would get me ready and drop me off at Grandma and Grandpa's house on Heard Avenue. It was still dark when I stepped into their warm kitchen, rubbing sleep out of my eyes while Grandma moved around in her robe, getting coffee ready. After dropping me off, Mom would head off to work. She worked at Wright-Patterson Air Force Base as a packaging specialist for the government. That's what it said on paper. But to me, she was just my hardworking mom doing everything she could to take care of us.

My grandparents' house became my second home. Grandma was everything you'd hope a grandma would be. She baked pies that filled the house with the scent of cinnamon and apples. Her cookies were soft, chewy, and always in a tin by the stove. She made cakes that melted in your mouth. In the summertime, we'd sit out back at the picnic table under the shade of the big tree. She'd slice up a watermelon, always the juiciest ones, and hand me a piece while I dangled my feet off the bench. I'd sit there eating quietly, listening to the birds, feeling safe.

As I got a little older, there was another reason I liked being at my grandparents' place: Marshall Thomas. He was four years older, like the big brother I didn't have. Marshall had a light-brown Impala with whitewalls, gangster walls, we called them. He kept it spotless. He'd wash it until the chrome shone, turn the radio up, and light a stick of incense. You could smell that car half a block away.

Other days I'd find him inside, ironing his jeans, pressing a crease so sharp it looked like it could cut. He stayed with his brother, Skip, and Skip's wife, Bertha. They let me hang around. When he finished, he'd nod toward the door and we'd start cruising Springfield. In the summer the porches were full and the sidewalks busy. Marshall knew where the girls were and they knew him. He was smooth, never in a hurry, always with a laugh.

Riding with Marshall felt like a little piece of freedom. I watched how he carried himself, how he kept his things in order, how he treated people. It was simple, but it mattered. That, too, was part of life in Springfield, Ohio.

Grandma was gentle, but she didn't play. She had her way of letting you know right from wrong. And she had a way of reading a situation without looking up from whatever she was doing. Grandpa, on the other hand, was the law. He was strict and didn't leave room for nonsense. When I stepped out of line, he didn't hesitate to correct me. He wasn't mean, but he was serious about discipline. If I did wrong, he'd let me know—sometimes with words, and sometimes with the belt. That's just how it was back then. He believed in order, structure, and setting a foundation. And to this day, I thank him for that.

He was a hard worker, too. He worked for International Harvester, driving brand-new trucks straight off the assembly line. He'd park one and head back to the front for another. It was a rhythm, a process. He did it with care and consistency. Grandpa had been in the military when he was younger. He brought that same precision into everything he did. He was half Filipino, half Black. His father had met his mother in the Philippines during the Spanish-American War. My great-grandfather was an American soldier who fell in love and stayed long enough to start a family. That's how Grandpa, Ernest Kenneth Smith, came to be.

There were more hands helping raise me than just my mom and grandparents. Mom had four sisters and two younger brothers. A big family meant there was always someone around, always someone ready to step in when needed. They helped me in small but meaningful ways. Each one left a mark on me.

Grandma, though, taught me how to be strong. I remember one moment like it happened yesterday. I was maybe nine or ten. There was a boy who'd been picking on me, not just him but a little group of boys who followed him around. I was tired of it. That day, Grandma was sitting out front in her favorite metal rocking chair under the tree. She was crocheting something. I stood nearby, hesitating, not sure what to do. She didn't even look up. She just said, "Go on and fight that boy."

I looked at her, surprised. She kept rocking, her fingers moving, eyes focused on her crochet hook.

"You don't let nobody push you around," she said.

So I did. Right there in the middle of the street, I squared up with that boy. I remember the noise, the shouting, fists flying, and the hot pavement beneath my feet. A bigger kid named Red, who lived just a couple of houses down, came running to break it up. He pulled us apart. I turned around and walked back up to the house, breathing heavily and scraped up.

Grandma didn't even look up. She just kept rocking, then said, "Go wash your hands and get ready for supper." That's what she called every meal—supper. Morning, noon, or night, it was always supper.

Faith was a big part of my upbringing, too. My grandparents were devoted Catholics. They believed in the rituals, the sacraments, the traditions. I was baptized Catholic and sent to St. Mary's, the local Catholic school. I wore the uniform, went to Mass, and sat in classrooms with nuns who didn't smile much. At first, it wasn't so bad. But as I got older, I started to feel boxed in. I started to test limits.

One day, I pushed too far. I got kicked out of St. Mary's. It wasn't just a suspension or a warning. They threw me out. I can still see the look on my grandpa's face when he found out. That was the day I got the last beating of my life.

I stood in the living room, nervous and shaking. Grandpa came in holding a belt, his face hard. He didn't say much. He didn't have to. The sting of that belt stayed with me, not just on my back, but in my memory. I was twelve years old, and I knew then that I had crossed a line I couldn't come back from. That was the last time I stepped that far out of line. The last time Grandpa had to lay a hand on me.

Looking back now, I see how each piece of that childhood shaped me. The tiny room with Mom, the morning drop-offs while it was still dark, the watermelon slices in the backyard, the fights in the street, the belt on my back, the lessons from Grandma's rocker. Each memory, whether it hurt or healed, left something behind. A scar, a story, a lesson.

Those days in Springfield weren't easy. We didn't have much. But we had love, discipline, structure, and family. We had the kind of roots that don't break when the wind blows. I didn't understand it then, but I do now. That tiny upstairs room and those creaky stairs weren't just a place I lived. They were the beginning of everything.

Springfield wasn't just where I was born. It was where I learned how to fight, how to cry, how to keep going. It was where I learned what mattered. Family. Pride. Respect. Getting up when you're knocked down. Washing your hands and showing up for supper, no matter what just happened out in the street.

Everything started there. And even now, I carry that place with me, not just in memory, but in how I live, how I love, and how I keep moving forward.

Chapter 2:
The Move to Yellow Springs

I'll never forget the night our house got hit by lightning. It was one of those summer evenings when the air feels electric and the sky flashes with angry streaks of light. My mom had just mentioned something strange. She said she could feel heat coming through the wall. It didn't seem right. Then we started to smell it. It was an awful, unmistakable scent of smoke. It wasn't just a scent. It crept into the room like a warning, subtle at first, then impossible to ignore.

Before we knew it, we were making our way downstairs to evacuate. As we reached the steps, a firefighter passed us, heading up into the danger we were trying to escape. I remember the way his boots pounded up the stairs, the heavy gear he wore, and the sense of calm urgency in his face. Everything was moving fast, but the moment felt frozen in my memory.

That night, we left behind the only home we knew. My mom and I moved in with my grandparents until we could figure out what came next. Their place became our temporary safe haven, full of warm meals and familiar voices. But we couldn't stay there forever. We needed a new beginning, and that beginning turned out to be in Yellow Springs.

Yellow Springs was only seven miles from Springfield, but it might as well have been a different world. The small village had just over four thousand people. It was surrounded by trees and filled with charm. There was something about the place that instantly felt alive. It was eclectic and quirky, the kind of town where creativity floated in the air. People described it as a little hippy village, and I could see why. It was the home of Antioch College, a liberal arts school known for being progressive and free-spirited. Rod Serling, the man behind *The Twilight Zone*, had once walked these streets as a student. Years later, Dave Chappelle would become one of the town's most recognizable faces. You could spot him skating around with his son or sitting casually on the steps of a local shop, puffing on a cigarette.

Living in Yellow Springs felt like stepping into a new chapter of life. I didn't know it then, but the people I would meet here would shape my life in countless ways. I quickly found my circle of friends who lived just blocks away and who would be part of my life through junior high and into high school.

Robert White, Aaron Blackman, and Terry Lawson became my closest friends. We did everything together. Terry, especially, was more than a friend. He was like a brother. His family welcomed me with open arms, and I felt completely at home in their house. Terry had two brothers, Gary and Jerry. Jerry was older, and Gary was younger, and I got along with both of them. Their parents were kind and warm, and I found myself spending a lot of time at their house. It wasn't just Terry I was close with—it was the whole Lawson family. They became my extended family in Yellow Springs.

By the time high school started, our group had expanded. That's when Deacon Sneed joined the crew. Deacon was from Dayton, and he brought a whole new energy to our circle. He was about five feet eleven, dark-skinned, and always had something to say. Deacon was the kind of guy who could make you laugh at the most unexpected times. We clicked right away.

One of the best things about Deacon was that he had a car. That changed everything. Now we could go to concerts and parties without begging our parents for rides. We made the most of it. Together, we saw acts like the Ohio Players, Earth, Wind & Fire, the Commodores, Zapp, and plenty more. The music felt like it was part of our lives, and every show we attended was a memory burned into our youth.

But Deacon's car wasn't exactly in perfect shape. I remember one night in particular, riding back from a party on a road called Devil's Backbone. That road was no joke— sharp curves, no lights, and if you went off the edge, it could be days before anyone found you. It was the middle of the night, probably around 2 a.m., and we were cruising along when we heard it.

Pop. Robert leaned forward. "Deac, I think you got a flat."

Deacon just nodded and said we'd pull over once we made it up the next hill. No sooner had he said that when we heard another pop. This time it was the back left tire. Then, just minutes later, a third tire blew. Three out of four tires were flat. The ride turned into a slow crawl. We rolled into

Yellow Springs doing about ten miles per hour, laughing and shaking our heads the whole way. My mom had warned him. She had seen those tires and called them bald retreads. She told Deacon to be careful, and she was right. We barely made it back.

Despite adventures like that, or maybe because of them, high school in Yellow Springs was a time I'll never forget. The school had a reputation for having some of the prettiest girls around. That was definitely true, and it made going to class a bit more exciting. But it wasn't all fun and games. The school also had a solid basketball team, a tough football squad, and a track team that held its own. Sports were a big part of our identity. They brought the school together and gave us something to rally around.

Still, not everything about high school was easy. One of the moments that really stuck with me was when I ended up in the principal's office. They had built a junior high school on the same property as the high school, and one day, during school hours, I decided to join a pickup basketball game. The problem was that junior high was still in session, and we weren't supposed to be out there.

Someone caught us and marched me straight to the high school principal's office. At the time, the principal was Mr. Newsome. I didn't know what to expect. What I got was a wake-up call.

That moment stayed with me, especially later on when I tried to get my report card and was told I couldn't receive it because I hadn't returned a textbook. I went to Mr.

Newsome again, asking if he could tell me my grades. He looked me in the eye and told me I had gotten all Ds and one C.

I was stunned. That hit me hard. I kept thinking about how my mom would react. She had already been through so much. We had lost our home. She was working hard to give me a stable life, and I was slacking off in school. That moment changed something in me.

I knew I had to do better.

From that point on, I started applying myself. It wasn't easy. Science was the class that gave me the most trouble. No matter how hard I tried, it always seemed just out of reach. I didn't hate it, but I struggled. I would read the assignments and still feel lost. The experiments, the formulas, all of it felt like a foreign language. But I kept going. I showed up. I asked questions. I studied more than I ever had. I had to. I didn't want another semester of bad grades. I wanted my mom to be proud of me.

It wasn't a sudden transformation. There were still days I fell behind or felt overwhelmed. But little by little, I improved. I stopped skating by and started actually learning. And that made all the difference.

Looking back, Yellow Springs gave me more than just a new home. It gave me a second chance. It gave me the kind of friends who felt like family. It gave me concerts and laughter and late-night drives with bald tires. It gave me the kind of memories that stick with you for life. Most of all, it gave me a reason to grow up.

I didn't get everything right in those years. I made mistakes. I learned some lessons the hard way. But I also found out what I was capable of. I found out that even when things fall apart, even when your house goes up in smoke, there's still a way forward. You just have to keep moving. Keep trying. Keep pushing.

Yellow Springs was that place for me. It held me up when the world felt like it was falling down. And for that, I'll always be grateful.

Chapter 3:
Track, Brotherhood, and College Life

I was a freshman when they asked me to come out for track. At Yellow Springs we weren't the biggest school, but we had speed that made people pay attention. Dorian Benning was the name everyone knew. He came from a fast family, his sister Gina was an athlete, and before any of us set foot in high school, his older brother, Butch, was already a story people told. Butch had been one of the top sprinters in Ohio, the kind of runner coaches still talked about years later.

The day of the big race is burned into my memory like it just happened yesterday. When our high school was finally called for the next heat, my nerves were already stretched tight. We walked out onto the track, each of us finding our lanes, and I remember glancing at the white tape that marked the spot where I was supposed to hand the baton to Ed. I tried to gauge the distance, making sure I had it locked in my mind. That little piece of tape meant everything in that moment. It was the line between success and disaster.

We had more than one anchor. John Gudgel, a true quarter-miler, was a junior and built for that race. Ed Rice ran with purpose and talked about heading to a military academy after graduation. Looking around at those guys, I understood I was stepping into something real. We might have been a small dot on the map, but in southwest Ohio we had some of the best.

Dorian used to talk about the Horseshoe in Columbus like it was a cathedral, how the state championships felt inside that place, a bowl big enough to hold close to a hundred thousand. The first time our bus rolled up to Ohio State and we walked through the tunnel, his words came back to me. The sound rose up and pressed against my chest. I felt small and electric at the same time, a freshman with a relay spot, trying to breathe steady and belong.

The stadium was packed, filled with the sound of people talking, laughing, and cheering. Yet for me, everything slowed down. The noise faded into the background, and it felt like I was moving through water. My focus was on the track, the curve ahead of me, and that baton in my hand. The official raised his voice and called out, "Runners, take your mark." My legs felt like stone, yet my heart was racing. Then he said, "Set." For a breathless moment the world froze.

BANG. The gun went off, and I exploded forward. My legs pumped, my arms drove hard, and I leaned into the run with everything I had. I didn't feel faster than anyone else, but I didn't feel slower either. My job was simple. Hold my ground. Don't let anyone blow past me. That was all I could think about.

As we rounded the curve, I spotted Ed waiting for me, already glancing back, getting ready for the handoff. He shifted on his feet, then took off, trusting I'd be right there. I stretched out the baton, reaching with all I had, but something felt wrong. I wasn't close enough. No matter how far I reached, the space between us seemed to grow. My fingers stretched, but the baton was just short of his hand.

Then it happened. I stumbled forward, the world tilting, and before I knew it, I hit the track face first. A loud groan rolled over the crowd, that kind of collective sound that makes your heart sink deeper than the pain in your body. My knee scraped badly against the track, burning hot and raw. I dared not lift my head. I didn't want to see the looks on my teammates' faces or the scoreboard that would confirm what I already knew.

We had finished dead last.

For a moment, I wished the track would just swallow me whole. But before the weight of it could crush me, I felt a hand on my shoulder. Dorian leaned down, calm as ever, and told me, "That's okay. Don't worry about it. You'll be back next year." His voice carried a reassurance I needed, even if I couldn't fully believe it yet. The other teammates didn't say anything. Maybe they didn't know what to say. Maybe they were just as stunned as I was.

Later, Dorian gave me advice that stuck. He said the best way to come back stronger was to spend the summer training, working out, and getting better. He believed in me, and for some reason, even though I had just failed so publicly, I believed in myself too.

That summer, heading into my sophomore year, I joined the Upward Bound program at Central State University. It was more than just classes and summer school.

Many inner-city kids from Dayton, Ohio were part of it, and a good number of them were athletes. Most came from majority Black high schools in Dayton, and they could flat out run. I wasn't there for summer courses. I was there for the track program.

Competing with those athletes was like stepping into a new world. These weren't kids from small schools like Yellow Springs. They were double A and triple A athletes, from schools much larger and with far more competition. The first time I lined up against them, I wasn't sure if I belonged. But as the weeks went on, something clicked. I dropped my times in the hundred to 9.9, then 9.8 seconds. Every tenth of a second felt like a victory.

It was during this time that I met athletes who would go on to become legends in their own right. Todd Bell was one of them. He later became a champion long jumper. Roland James was another. He went to the University of Tennessee and eventually played football for them before moving on to the New England Patriots. Roland was a good guy, humble despite his talent. We'd talk whenever we saw each other, whether it was during the summer programs or later at track meets. Being around athletes like that made me push myself harder.

I also got a taste of AAU track and field during the summers. That world was fierce, but I managed to place in the sprints. For me, high school would never be the same after that. I returned to Yellow Springs stronger, faster, and more confident. Suddenly, I wasn't just another runner. I was dominating the sprints. At meets, I became the guy who would run the hundred, the two hundred, and the four hundred, tripling almost every time. It was exhausting, but it was also thrilling to know I could pull it off.

By my junior year, my coach was Tim McLinden. He had a pretty laid-back style, not one to hover too much, but he was a good man and a solid coach. That year he took me to Columbus to run the sixty-yard dash indoors against some of the state's top sprinters. Running indoors was new to me, but it was the perfect way to jumpstart my season. I finished second place and even managed to get a little article in the news. Seeing my name in print, even in a small write-up, did wonders for my confidence.

That entire year, I dominated the sprints. I became a kind of show at the track meets. People came to watch, and I knew eyes were on me every time I stepped on the line. Coach McLinden still had me running the quarter mile too, partly to develop me, but truth be told, the quarter really belonged to one guy, and that was John Gudgel. John was a beast when it came to that race. We both knew it. The quarter was his domain, and he owned it.

The thing about John was that he wasn't a trash talker. He didn't need to be. He just lined up, ran his race, and left everyone else chasing him. Together, he and I became the backbone of our team's success. Between my dominance in the sprints and his strength in the quarter mile, we were untouchable.

We rolled through the sectional championships and then the districts at Welcome Stadium in Dayton, Ohio. Each step took us closer to the big stage. Eventually, we found ourselves back in Columbus, standing in the Horseshoe at Ohio State, ready for the state championships.

That meet was unforgettable. John crushed the quarter mile, living up to every expectation. I pulled out the win in the hundred-yard dash. Our victories stacked points for Yellow Springs, and soon it became clear that we were not just winning individual races. We were chasing something bigger. Our combined efforts led Yellow Springs High School to its first ever state title. When it was all over, we stood together in the newspaper, smiling, holding the championship trophy.

That year, John earned a scholarship to the University of Toledo for track. He proved himself to be one of the best at the university level, just as everyone expected. As for me, my journey was still unfolding.

By my senior year, the rhythm was almost routine. I kept winning, and every Monday morning after a meet, I'd stop by the principal's office to see if there was a letter waiting for me. Colleges from all over were reaching out. It became a part of my life. Check the mail, see who was interested, then head to the library to research schools. I would pull out the Barron's book of colleges and study the options, circling schools that caught my eye.

I wasn't content to wait for opportunities to come to me. I started writing letters myself, attaching articles and track results, sending them out to schools. It was my way of making sure they knew I existed. Coming from a small school like Yellow Springs, I couldn't assume they had ever heard of me. I wanted to go out of state. I wanted to prove myself on a bigger stage.

Most of the schools I wrote to replied. That alone felt good, but one stood out above the rest. Western Michigan University in Kalamazoo kept showing the most interest. Their coach, Oren Richberg, reached out, and soon they invited me to check out the campus.

Western Michigan had everything I wanted. They were Division I, part of the Mid-American Conference, and had nearly thirty thousand students. It was the kind of school where I could compete at the highest level while also experiencing college life to its fullest.

Then came the day I had been waiting for. A letter of intent arrived. This was the real thing. Signing it meant I was committed to Western Michigan. It meant they would cover tuition, room, and board. All I had to do was put my name on the line, and my future was set. I returned for my senior year with even more determination. That spring, I won both the hundred and the two hundred at the state championships. My high school journey ended on the highest note possible.

That fall, I packed up my dreams and headed to Western Michigan University. I planned to major in Communications with a minor in Public Administration. But more than anything, I was going there to run track, to take everything I had learned and earned and prove myself at the next level. It was a new chapter, full of promise, and I couldn't wait to get started.

Chapter 4:
Western Michigan Beginnings

When I arrived at Western Michigan University, I knew that track and field would be my anchor. From the start, I could feel the energy of the program, and it was clear I had stepped into a world that would push me both physically and mentally. Coach Jack Shaw had a reputation for recruiting strong athletes and building teams that could compete with some of the best in the nation. He had an eye for talent, and before long, he pulled together a group of sprinters who would shape my college years in ways I could not have imagined.

There were four of us who became a unit. Alongside me was Lawrence Claxton from Detroit. Lawrence was already well-known back home. He had earned the recognition of being an All-City sprinter, a mark of distinction that showed just how dominant he was in his area. His specialty was the 100-meter dash, and he was built for speed. Lawrence carried himself with confidence, but not in a way that pushed people away. He had a sharp laugh and an easy-going nature that made training with him enjoyable.

The second was Warren Miller, who came from Camden, New Jersey. Warren was not only a sprinter but also a talented long jumper. He had that rare combination of explosive power and agility, and his ability to shift from the sprint to the jump pit was something to admire. He was competitive, always pushing himself to improve, and in turn, he pushed the rest of us. Warren brought a quiet determination to the group. He was not the loudest voice, but his presence carried weight.

Then there was Michael Lockhart from Akron, Ohio. Michael had a way of blending speed with endurance, making him a reliable runner in many different events. He had a serious focus when it came to training, but off the track, he was lighthearted and quick to joke. Together, the four of us formed the backbone of our sprint squad. Coach Shaw had plans for us individually, but he also knew what we could do together.

That was how we came to form a relay team. Running the relay was more than just a race. It was about timing, trust, and rhythm. Passing the baton required precision, and with each practice we grew more confident in one another. We learned how to anticipate movements, how to read each other's speed, and how to run not as individuals but as one unit. That trust showed in our performances.

Our hard work paid off when we won the American Conference Championship and the Central Collegiate Conference Championship. Those victories remain some of the proudest moments of my athletic career. Standing with my teammates on the podium, knowing we had fought together and come out on top, gave me a deep sense of pride. Track was demanding, but it gave me a sense of purpose and belonging during those four years.

College, however, was not just about athletics. I managed to balance the demands of training, traveling, and studying and graduated in four years with a degree in

Communications. That degree meant something to me. It was proof that I could remain disciplined and committed not only on the track but also in the classroom. School itself was fun, and I made the most of it. I made great friends, found ways to enjoy myself, and got involved in activities that went far beyond track.

Some of the best experiences came from traveling to major meets across the country. Competing at these events exposed me to a higher level of competition and allowed me to see some of the greatest athletes of that era. We traveled to the Drake Relays, a meet that always drew some of the top talent. I remember watching Herschel Walker there. To see him in person was like watching a different breed of athlete altogether. His power and speed were unmatched.

At the Penn Relays in Philadelphia, the atmosphere was electric. Crowds filled the stadium, and the energy was contagious. That was where I saw Ronaldo Nehemiah run. He was a world-class hurdler, and the way he attacked the hurdles was something to behold. Smooth, powerful, and fast, he made it look effortless, though I knew how much work went into his performance.

We also went down to Knoxville, Tennessee, for the Dogwood Relays. That was where I lined up against Willie Gault. Running against him was eye-opening. He had speed that felt almost impossible to catch. In those same meets, I also witnessed the raw ability of Carl Lewis, who at that time was redefining what sprinting and jumping looked like. Watching him run and jump gave me inspiration and showed me what the peak of the sport truly was.

Coach Jack Shaw played a big role in making sure we had those opportunities. He worked hard to get us into top meets across the country, and his dedication as a coach helped us stay prepared. He was tough but fair, and I always felt he wanted the best for us. Under his guidance, we improved not only as athletes but as individuals.

During my time at Western, another experience shaped me just as much as track. I had the chance to join a fraternity. The fraternity was Phi Delta Psi, and it was relatively new at the time. Despite being young, it was growing at a phenomenal rate. Within its first four or five years, the fraternity had already built a strong presence, and by the time I joined, we had close to thirty brothers on the yard.

What made Phi Delta Psi different was that it did not carry the same long history as some of the older historically Black fraternities like the Kappas or the Alphas. Instead, it was fresh, full of energy, and attracting young men who wanted to build something of their own. The fraternity had ten founders, and we were only the third line to cross into the organization. The first line called themselves 1/5 of Phi. The second was known as the Five Noble Knights. Then came us, the Hard Time 9. Being part of that third line gave us a sense of pride. We were laying the groundwork for the future of Phi Delta Psi.

I grew to love those brothers. They became family to me, and the bond we formed went beyond college. Our president was Dennis Jones, who also happened to be one of the original founders. Dennis was not tall, but his leadership was powerful. He had first come to Western as a wrestler, but an injury ended his athletic career. Instead of leaving, he stayed to focus on his education.

Dennis ran our meetings with precision, always following Robert's Rules of Order. At the time, I did not fully appreciate what that discipline meant, but later I understood how important it was to have a leader who valued structure and respect. Dennis set a standard for all of us. Many of the younger brothers, including myself, looked to him as a role model. He graduated with a degree in Business and went on to work for IBM, where he quickly rose to become one of the top account executives in the company nationally. Later, he continued his career at Hewlett-Packard before starting his own company. His path showed us what was possible when discipline and vision came together.

There were many other brothers in Phi Delta Psi who went on to do impressive things. Charles Redd was one of them. Charles graduated and began working with Coca-Cola, holding management roles in the consumer industry. Over time, he shifted into a new path and became a pastor and motivational speaker. His life took on a different mission, one focused on inspiring others. He even went on to write a book that reflected his journey and lessons learned. His story was one of transformation and purpose, and it inspired many of us.

Being part of the Hard Time 9 was about more than fraternity rituals or campus events. It was about building bonds that carried through life. We supported each other, held each other accountable, and celebrated each other's victories. In many ways, the fraternity balanced what I had on the track team. One gave me competition and athletic discipline, while the other gave me brotherhood and personal growth.

When I look back on those four years at Western, I see them as some of the most formative years of my life. Track and field gave me a stage to push my body and my mind to their limits. Traveling to the big meets gave me exposure to greatness, and competing at a high level gave me confidence that I carried into other areas of life. At the same time, joining Phi Delta Psi gave me lifelong brothers and role models who showed me how to succeed beyond athletics.

Graduating in four years with my degree in Communications was the achievement that tied it all together. It was proof that I had managed to balance it all. School, sports, and fraternity life blended into an experience that I would carry with me long after I left campus. Western Michigan University was not just a stop along the way. It was a foundation. It was where I learned discipline, built friendships, and became part of something larger than myself.

Looking back now, I realize that the combination of athletics, academics, and fraternity life created a balance that shaped me into the person I became. Each part had its role, and together they made my college years unforgettable.

Chapter 5:
Life at Western Michigan

There were so many sharp guys in our fraternity. From the moment I pledged, I could see that it was a gathering place for men who carried themselves with confidence. Everyone seemed to have something special about them. Some were athletes, some were scholars, and others were natural leaders who knew how to take command of a room. I learned a lot just by being around them. They weren't perfect, but they challenged me to sharpen myself and to hold my head up high in whatever I did. Being surrounded by men like that made college life feel both exciting and competitive.

Alongside fraternity life, I took on an internship that turned out to be one of the most eye-opening experiences of my college years. I had the opportunity to work for Congressman Howard Whoope, who represented Kalamazoo. For a full quarter, I spent my afternoons and evenings in his office, answering phones, writing down the concerns of citizens, and sitting in on discussions about local issues. It was a lot more responsibility than I expected. People called with real problems. Some were upset about taxes, others about jobs, and some about schools or housing. My role was to listen carefully and record their concerns so they could be addressed. It might not have been glamorous, but it gave me a window into how government functioned at the ground level.

I remember one woman calling several times a week about her neighborhood park. She said it had become a place for troublemakers at night, and she wanted the city to light it better. She wasn't yelling or making demands, but you could hear the worry in her voice. She wanted her kids to be safe. I wrote her complaint down carefully every time. Experiences like that made me realize how important it was for leaders to listen to the everyday voices of people who trusted them to make things better. I did not know if her park was ever fixed, but I knew that my notes were part of the chain of communication that gave her a chance to be heard.

The internship made me feel like I was part of something bigger. I was just a young college student, but there I was, sitting inside the office of a Congressman, trying to make sure I represented the people of Kalamazoo the right way. It showed me that no matter how big or small the task, it mattered when it came to serving others. That lesson stayed with me long after I left that office.

But the most important thing that happened to me at Western Michigan was not in the classroom or even through politics. It was on the campus grounds one afternoon when I first saw Kim Brooks. She was walking across campus with purpose, as if she had somewhere important to be. She was petite, graceful, and carried herself with confidence. Her long brown hair caught the light, and her eyes held a beauty that was hard to look away from. I remember standing there, just watching her, feeling as if time slowed down. In that moment, I knew I had to meet her.

Being in a fraternity had its advantages, so I asked one of the pledges to get her information for me. He came back with her name and a little bit of background. She was from Detroit, and people called her Ty. That was her nickname, and it seemed to fit her perfectly. She had that city edge to her. She was smart, confident, and had a toughness that came from growing up in Detroit. I tried to make a move and even asked her out on a date. She stood me up. Most guys would have been discouraged, but I could see from the beginning that she was not going to make things easy. That made her even more attractive.

Kim had a presence that set her apart. She was pretty, no doubt about that, but her intelligence and street smarts gave her a sharpness that drew me in. She was feisty, quick to speak her mind, and she did not let anyone push her around. People saw me as the country boy, raised with small-town values and a quieter way of moving through life. She was the city girl, bold and direct. On the surface, we were complete opposites, but deep down I knew we could balance each other in ways that would make us strong. Later in life, we would become a formidable pair. But at that time, I was just a young man trying to win the heart of a woman who was not easily impressed.

Western Michigan University was about four hours from my hometown of Yellow Springs, Ohio. The drive was long enough that I felt independent but close enough that I could still visit home if I needed to. The first time I stepped on campus, I was impressed by how welcoming it felt. My dorm room was small, but it was mine, and I had all the basics to settle in. The orientation packet they handed out was thick with information about classes, clubs, and sports facilities. One thing that stood out right away was the indoor track facility. I had never seen anything like it before. The fact that we could run indoors all winter long meant that training would never stop. For a runner like me, that was perfect.

The coaching staff shaped my athletic journey in big ways. Oren Richburg was our coach at first, but soon after I arrived he left to take a head coaching job at another university. That left Jack Shaw in charge. Coach Shaw had been the head coach at Western Michigan for over twenty-one years, and you could tell right away that he knew what he was doing. He had a calm authority and a way of earning respect without raising his voice. He expected hard work, but he also knew how to guide us through challenges.

Coach Shaw made a smart decision by bringing in Halbert Bates as the sprint coach. Bates had been a sprinter at Western himself, so he understood not only the physical demands but also the mindset needed to succeed. He was all business. Every day he came prepared with a workout schedule written clearly on the board. There was no guessing what we were going to do. The drills were tough. Stairs, hills, and repeated sprint work pushed us to our limits, but Bates had a way of showing us that the pain would pay off. He believed in his sprinters, and because of that, we believed in him.

Over time, the sprinters became more than just teammates. They became my brothers. We spent so many hours sweating, pushing through exhaustion, and cheering each other on that we built a bond that felt like family. If one of us struggled, the others lifted him up. If one of us celebrated, we all celebrated together. It was that kind of environment that made me not only a stronger runner but also a stronger person.

The following year, our sprinting group grew even larger. We recruited a whole new wave of talent, including a hurdler named Carl Buchanan. Carl had a natural rhythm over the hurdles and brought an energy that was contagious. We also brought in James Williams, a sprinter from Gary, Indiana. James was fast and hungry to prove himself. With each new addition, our team felt more complete. We pushed each other to be better, and every practice felt like a test of will and determination.

Looking back, those days at Western Michigan shaped me in ways I could not have predicted. I had the structure of athletics, the challenges of academics, and the lessons of leadership from both my fraternity and my internship. And in the middle of it all, I was chasing the heart of a girl who would one day change my life. The mix of experiences made that period of my life unforgettable.

At the time, it was not always clear how all the pieces would fit together. I just knew I was learning, growing, and being shaped by the people around me. College was not just about books and classrooms. It was about the late nights with teammates, the endless drills on the track, the calls I answered in a Congressman's office, and the persistence it took to try to win over Kim. It was about building a foundation for the man I was becoming.

And though I did not know it yet, every single part of it, from the sprints to the politics to the moments on campus when I caught sight of Kim walking by, would play a role in preparing me for the future.

Chapter 6:
College Graduation

The day of my college graduation arrived, and it felt like the closing of one book and the opening of another. The morning was filled with excitement, nerves, and that unmistakable sense that something important was about to happen. I woke up earlier than usual, even before the alarm clock had the chance to ring. I lay in bed for a few minutes, letting the reality of the day sink in. After years of lectures, late-night study sessions, term papers, and exams, this was it. Today I would walk across the stage, shake a hand, and receive a diploma that carried more weight than the paper it was printed on.

My grandparents came to celebrate with me. Their presence meant everything because they had always been steady anchors in my life. They represented tradition, stability, and unconditional love. My mother was there too, beaming with pride, her smile lighting up every corner of the room we gathered in before the ceremony. She had been my strongest supporter throughout college, reminding me that hard work always paid off. My father even flew in from Los Angeles for the occasion. Seeing him there was a mixture of emotions. He had not always been present in my day-to-day life, but the fact that he made the effort to show up spoke volumes. For me, having both of my parents together, along with my grandparents, turned the day into something unforgettable.

The graduation ceremony itself was a blur of speeches, names being called, and the sound of applause echoing through the auditorium. I remember walking across the stage, my cap balanced on my head, my gown swaying with each step. When my name was announced, it felt like the world stopped for a moment. I shook hands with the dean, accepted the diploma, and glanced toward the audience. My family was clapping, cheering, and even wiping away tears. For all the long nights and the challenges I had faced during those years, this was the reward. This was the moment that validated every ounce of effort.

Afterward, we gathered for photos, laughter, and memories that would last a lifetime. My mother hugged me tightly and whispered that she was proud. My father clapped me on the back and told me this was just the beginning. My grandparents looked at me like I had climbed the tallest mountain, their pride shining in their eyes. It was one of those rare days when everything aligned and life seemed full of possibilities.

When the celebrations ended and the caps were tossed, life shifted back to its normal rhythm. I returned home, and for the first time in years, I had no assignments waiting, no exams on the horizon. The freedom felt strange. I allowed myself a little time to rest, to breathe, and to reflect. I slept in some mornings, lingered over breakfast, and spent quiet afternoons thinking about what I wanted next. But rest could not last forever. I knew that the next step was to find a job.

My mother had a friend who worked in the construction industry. Through that connection, she was able to secure a temporary job for me. It was not glamorous, and it certainly was not what I had envisioned after college, but it was a paycheck. I needed to earn money, and I needed to start somewhere. The job was on the freeway, working with hot asphalt and heavy equipment. I still remember my first day on the site, the sun beating down and the smell of tar filling the air. It was hard labor, unlike anything I had ever experienced.

I was given a tamper, a heavy tool used to press the asphalt into place. My task was to flatten it out, making sure the roadbed was even and solid. The work was repetitive, physically demanding, and unforgiving. The heat rose from the ground as we poured the asphalt, and by midday it felt like standing in an oven. My clothes were soaked with sweat, my arms ached, and my back throbbed from the strain. But there was a strange kind of pride in it. I was earning my pay through sheer effort, the kind of work that left your body sore but your spirit toughened.

My mornings began before the sun had fully risen. My mother would drop me off in Dayton, where I caught a bus heading toward the construction site. From there, I would hop onto the back of a truck with the other workers. The ride out was noisy and dusty, and we all braced ourselves for the long day ahead. At the end of each shift, I caught a ride back into the city, then hitchhiked my way home to Yellow Springs. It was a routine that required grit and endurance, but it became my life for that month.

I was being paid $11.87 an hour, which at the time felt like a decent wage, especially for someone fresh out of college. I would count my money at the end of the week and feel a sense of accomplishment. I was earning my way, proving that I could work hard and survive on my own. Yet deep down, I knew this was not the path I wanted to follow forever.

The job also opened my eyes to a world I was not fully part of. Most of the men I worked alongside had never gone to college. They were tough, hardened by years of labor, and their views of the world were different from mine. Many were small-town guys who had grown up working with their hands, and some carried rough edges that made me stand out. They called me the college boy. I tried to fit in, but there was always a quiet reminder that I was different. Conversations at lunch breaks often left me silent, listening more than speaking. I respected them, but I knew I did not belong in that life for the long haul.

After about a month, a union representative came to the site. They wanted me to join, but membership required several hundred dollars in dues. That was money I did not have, and even if I did, I was not sure I wanted to invest it in a future I could not see myself embracing. I was already feeling restless, knowing that pouring asphalt could not be the culmination of four years of college. I wanted more, and I needed to find it.

During this time, I spoke often with my father. He was living in Los Angeles, and the idea of California carried with it a sense of opportunity and reinvention. He encouraged me to come out and try my luck there. His words planted a seed that grew stronger with each passing day on the construction site. I imagined palm trees, city lights, and a different kind of future. I thought about the career I wanted to build and how unlikely it was to be found on the side of a freeway with a tamper in hand.

By September of 1981, my decision was made. I packed my belongings into a Foot Locker trunk, the kind you could lock with a heavy latch. It held everything I owned that mattered. Clothes, books, a few personal treasures, and the dreams I carried. I bought a ticket for the first bus headed west, determined to start over in Los Angeles.

The morning I left was bittersweet. My mother hugged me tightly, her eyes filled with both pride and worry. She wanted me to succeed but hated the thought of me being so far away. My grandparents gave me their blessing, reminding me to stay grounded and work hard. I promised to write and call as often as I could.

As the bus pulled away, I watched the familiar streets of Yellow Springs fade into the distance. I thought about the graduation ceremony, the construction job, the sweat, the long rides, and the people I had met along the way. All of it felt like preparation for this moment. I was leaving behind the safety of home and stepping into a future that was uncertain, but also wide open.

California was calling, and I was ready to answer.

Chapter 7:
Arriving In La La Land

The flight had been a little over three hours, and as the plane began its slow descent into the Los Angeles area, I pressed my forehead against the small oval window, eager to take it all in. The view below was nothing like Dayton, Ohio, where I had grown up. Down there, the land was flat and familiar, but this was another world entirely. First, I saw the tall buildings downtown, sparkling in the sun like something from a movie set. Beyond that, the mountains framed the horizon, rugged and majestic, nothing like the rolling hills back home. As we dropped lower, I noticed something else. It seemed like every other house had a swimming pool glistening in the sunlight. From up here, the blue rectangles looked like jewels scattered across the endless neighborhoods.

It hit me in that moment. I was in Los Angeles. For a kid from Yellow Springs, this felt like stepping into a dream. Within minutes, the plane touched down, the wheels squealing against the runway. The stewardess's voice came over the intercom, cheerful and polished, "Welcome to Los Angeles. The temperature is eighty-two degrees. Enjoy your stay."

Eighty-two degrees. Back home, the weather could never promise something like that in late spring. I leaned back in my seat, grinning to myself. This was not just a trip. This could possibly be my new home.

When I walked out of the terminal, I immediately spotted my father. He stood there with a trimmed goatee, wearing sunglasses, looking every bit like the cool, confident man I remembered. That was Pop. He had grown up in Inkster, Michigan, gone on to Central State University, and then finished his undergrad and later his master's at Cal State Dominguez Hills. He was now an English teacher, sharp, stylish, and proud of it. My parents had never married, but they had kept a good relationship, and for that I was grateful.

I dragged my bag toward him, and he smiled before giving me a hug. Then, with a little flair, he led me to his car. It was a 1965 silver convertible Mustang, completely restored. The paint gleamed under the California sun, and the chrome sparkled so bright it almost blinded me. Inside, the seats were spotless, the dashboard polished, and when he turned the key, the engine purred with the kind of smooth growl only a classic car could give. I was already impressed.

We left the airport and headed down La Cienega Boulevard. With the top down, the warm breeze whipped across my face. As we drove, I looked far off into the distance and saw the Hollywood Hills. And then, there it was, perched high and bold against the hillsides, the Hollywood sign. I had seen it a thousand times in movies and on TV, but nothing compared to seeing it in person. "Damn," I whispered under my breath. This was slick. This was unreal.

Pop lived on the south side of town, near 29th and Normandy, in a small single-story home. On the drive there, he began showing me pieces of Los Angeles, pointing out neighborhoods, explaining how the city worked. LA wasn't like New York, with its crowded blocks stacked with people. It was vast, spread out, almost like a collection of small cities stitched together. I quickly understood there was going to be a lot to learn.

At the time, Pop taught English at a Los Angeles City College. He had always been a man who appreciated looking sharp, so one of the first places he introduced me to was a shop downtown in the Garment District called Mike's. It was a tailor shop where you could get fitted for a suit and have it perfectly tailored in about an hour. That was LA for you. Fast, polished, and full of options.

One of the first things I noticed about Los Angeles was its landscape. Palm trees lined the streets, tall and short, swaying in the breeze. They were everywhere, a part of the city's identity, and so different from anything I had ever seen in Ohio. And then there were the cars. Back home, the roads were filled with Chevys, Toyotas, and Fords. Here, those cars were around, but they blended with something else. Mercedes. BMWs. Audis. Ferraris. Lamborghinis. Rolls-Royces. You name it, and it seemed like it cruised these streets. Almost instantly, I became fascinated. Cars became one of my favorite things to look out for. Every drive promised something new.

Pop explained that if you kept driving west long enough, the city opened up to the Pacific Ocean. That was when I first learned about Venice Beach. He told me it was a place full of characters, artists, hippies, and dreamers. When I finally saw it for myself, I understood. Venice wasn't like anywhere else I had ever been. The boardwalk was alive with merchants selling jewelry, paintings, and trinkets. Musicians filled the air with sound, and the crowds were a melting pot of every nationality. It reminded me of Yellow Springs, not in its look but in the free-spirited vibe of the people.

To think that I was actually going to live here. Los Angeles would quickly become my city. The Lakers, the Dodgers, the Rams. The city of champions.

One morning, Pop tossed me the keys to his Mustang. He gave me directions to Venice Beach and told me to take a drive. The first thing I noticed every time I stepped outside was the difference in the air. Back in Ohio, the air carried the scent of farmland and cow manure. Here, it smelled like fresh bread from a bakery, or grilled food from a street vendor. Flowers bloomed in the gardens near USC, and the rose garden east of campus filled the air with sweetness. The city had a heartbeat. You could feel it in the smells, the sounds, the movement all around you.

With the top down and a local hip-hop station playing through the speakers, I cruised north toward the Wilshire District. The Wilshire Center looked like downtown, but it wasn't. Pop had told me the difference, but I still marveled at how the city was divided into so many districts, each with its own character. I passed Hancock Park, where lawns were carefully manicured, and mansions stretched behind iron gates. Fremont Place was tucked in there too, a gated community where celebrities like

Muhammad Ali and Lou Rawls had once lived. It was a different level of living.

Continuing down Wilshire Boulevard, I rolled into the Miracle Mile, where tall buildings loomed and art museums stood proudly. If you turned north on almost any street here, you would eventually run into Hollywood. But I kept heading west. Soon, I was in Beverly Hills. The name itself carried a weight, and seeing it in person was surreal. Ferraris and Rolls-Royces were not rare sights here. In fact, I saw so many Mercedes on the road that I half-joked to myself that they must be mass-produced in someone's garage. But no, this was just the reality of a wealthy city.

Farther along, I passed through Westwood, home of UCLA. Students filled the streets, and the village buzzed with life. Beyond that was Brentwood, where O.J. Simpson lived at the time. Mansions sprawled across the hillsides, each one seemingly larger than the last.

Finally, I reached Santa Monica. The ocean breeze carried through the car, and I could feel the salt in the air. Santa Monica had its own downtown, quieter than some of the other places, but full of charm. I turned left on Lincoln Boulevard, then right on Rose Street, and before long, I was at Venice Beach. I couldn't find parking, so I tucked the Mustang into an alley parallel to the boardwalk.

Venice Beach was alive. Street performers played drums, guitars, and horns. Artists painted right there on the sidewalks. Vendors sold incense, jewelry, and homemade crafts. Muscle Beach stood out, where bodybuilders pushed iron in the open air, their muscles glistening in the sun. Skaters and rollerbladers zipped past, weaving between the crowds. Everywhere I turned, the smell of cannabis mixed with grilled food and incense. The music came from all directions, reggae here, rock there, hip hop further down.

Before that trip, I had met Pop's girlfriend, Marie. She was a beautiful woman from New Orleans, dark-skinned with striking features and a soft accent. She worked for the airlines and often traveled to Maui to visit her sister. She had two daughters, Maria and Angel, who might someday become my stepsisters. One time, she had brought back a little stash of cannabis from Hawaii. She handed it to me and told me to roll a couple of joints, then keep the rest. That day, I slipped some into my pocket before heading out.

I found a spot on the sand, pulled off my shirt, and stretched out. Around me, people lounged, played volleyball, or roller-skated by. I put on my Walkman, a must-have back then, and tuned into Missing Persons, their hit "Walking in LA" pumping through the foam headphones. The sun beat down, but the ocean breeze kept me cool, the perfect balance. I lit up one of the joints Marie had given me and let the smoke drift into the air. In that moment, lying on the sand with the music, the sun, and the waves, I felt euphoric.

At some point, I wandered to a phone booth and called Mom. No cell phones back then, just quarters and a dial tone. She picked up, and I told her about the weather, the sights, the energy of the city. Then I told her the truth. "I'm not coming back," I said. "I'm going to find a job here.

This is where I'm going to stay." She listened, probably not surprised, but she reminded me how much she loved the changing seasons back home. I laughed and told her it never snowed here.

As I hung up, a man in all white skated past me on rollerblades. He had a turban on his head, an electric guitar strapped to his back, and a speaker blaring Hendrix. He shredded while weaving through the crowd, becoming part of the spectacle that was Venice Beach.

Los Angeles was already shaping me. Every day felt like an adventure. Before GPS, you had to learn your way with a Thomas Guide, a thick book that broke the city into quadrants. I kept one in the passenger seat of the Mustang, flipping through pages as I explored, memorizing the streets, piecing the city together one drive at a time. Slowly, I became comfortable, confident, and at home.

Los Angeles would be my city. From that first flight, through the drives on Wilshire, the days on the sand at Venice, and the endless discoveries of each district, I knew. This wasn't just a visit. This was the start of my life here, and I never looked back.

Chapter 8:
Moving To The Pharmaceutical Industry

In the fall of 1982, life began to take a new shape for me in California. I had landed a position on the UCLA campus, working in the school and art supplies department. It was not glamorous—retail never is—but it paid fifteen thousand a year and gave me stability. My title, assistant supervisor at the student store, sounded better than it felt. Most of my days were spent managing the stockroom and overseeing student employees. The work kept me busy and taught me responsibility, but I knew from the start it was not where I wanted to end up.

Still, I was proud of myself. I was on my feet in Los Angeles. I even bought a burnt orange Mazda 626, sporty enough to give me independence. Before that, I had taken the bus every day from my Mid-Wilshire apartment to UCLA. Those long rides were tiring but gave me time to watch the city and its people. On one of those final rides, I noticed a man sitting toward the back. It was Houston McTear, once the fastest man in the world with a 9.0-second hundred-yard dash. A world-class sprinter, just riding the bus like everyone else. I introduced myself, shook his hand, and found him humble and friendly. That moment stuck with me. It showed me Los Angeles would give me chances to meet people I had only read about or seen on TV. Encounters like that became routine later, but in those early days, it felt magical.

UCLA came with small perks. The campus was like its own little village filled with shops and restaurants. On lunch breaks I often sat outside, eating and people-watching. Beautiful women were everywhere—Black, white, Asian, Latina—stylish and confident. Los Angeles had a reputation for beautiful people, and UCLA lived up to it every single day. I often reminded myself that if you lost focus in a city like this, it could swallow you whole.

The best part of the job wasn't the work but the exposure. I dealt with sales reps from companies like Parker Pen and Stratford Paper, who supplied the store. They came in sharp suits, polished shoes, and easy smiles, moving with confidence. I asked them about their jobs and learned they worked for big companies, earned good salaries and bonuses, and drove company cars with expense accounts. They had freedom, independence, and all the perks of a solid career. That struck me. I thought, this is the kind of job I want. That was the first spark that drew me toward the pharmaceutical industry.

Meanwhile, my personal life mattered just as much. During the summer of 1982, I was still writing letters to Kim. I had made up my mind. I wanted to marry her and bring her to California. She pictured Los Angeles as one giant beach, but I knew she would quickly see it was far more. This was the second-largest city in the country, and if California were its own nation, its economy would rank among the biggest in the world. I promised her I would return, marry her, and build a life together in Los Angeles.

Some people doubted me, assuming I would never go back for her. But they were wrong. Our wedding wasn't extravagant, but it was meaningful. Surrounded by close friends and family in a church in Detroit, we exchanged vows and started our new chapter. Afterward, I brought Kim with me to Los Angeles. She didn't complain about the tiny apartment, the foldout bed, or the sparse furniture. She took it in stride. Before long, she landed a retail job at Joseph Magnin in Century City. Her commission structure sometimes gave her the chance to out-earn me, but together we made a strong team. With both incomes, we upgraded to a one-bedroom apartment just a few blocks away in Mid-Wilshire.

I'll never forget our first attempt at a nice dinner in Los Angeles. We showed up at a place we thought would be good, only to be turned away because we didn't have reservations. Lesson learned. In this city, you planned ahead if you wanted a seat anywhere special.

Not long after we settled in, my fraternity brothers began making their way west. John Green, my old roommate and closest friend, arrived first. Then came Andre Dawson, "The Duke," who achieved his dream of joining the LAPD. Another brother, Greg Kimball, had studied engineering and came to interview with California Edison. We had pledged at different times, but we became close after he moved to California.

Since Kim often worked Saturdays, Greg and I spent weekends exploring. One of our favorite drives was up Beverly Drive in Beverly Hills, which turned into Coldwater

Canyon and dropped into Studio City. Sometimes it beat the freeway. Laurel Canyon was another route we loved. Halfway up was a small liquor store with a neighborhood feel. It sold beer, wine, sandwiches, and odds and ends. We always stopped there before continuing.

Greg drove a Camaro, and many afternoons we grabbed a six-pack, drove up Mulholland Drive, and parked at the overlooks. From there the city stretched out below us, the lights flickering on as the sun dipped behind the hills. We'd raise our bottles, look over Los Angeles, and say, "We're here." Those moments made anything feel possible.

We also found a barbecue joint on Sunset Boulevard where we could sit outside, order peel-and-eat shrimp and barbecue chicken, and wash it down with tequila shots. Half the fun was people-watching, soaking in the city's energy. Every weekend felt like an adventure.

Another ritual was driving down Sepulveda Boulevard to the beach communities. Hermosa, Manhattan, and Redondo Beach became regular spots. Along the way, we passed rows of dealerships selling shiny BMWs, Porsches, and Mercedes. It was hard not to dream of owning one. At Redondo Beach, we discovered a small bar where we sat with beers in hand, grateful for the weather and the life we were building.

After our outings, I often swung by Century City to pick up Kim, and then she and I planned our evenings together. That rhythm became part of our life. Even in the fall and winter, the sun stayed bright and the days warm.

Other weekends I spent time with more fraternity brothers. Ray Frye, Carlton Goodall, and Jeff Dudley often organized racquetball games in Studio City. We worked up a sweat on the courts and caught up afterward, keeping the bond alive from our college days.

There was also Jay Jackson, another close friend who had taken over my old job at UCLA. Originally from Cleveland, Jay was a few years older, someone I looked up to like a big brother. He had married a UCLA student, and we often spent time with them too.

Piece by piece, Los Angeles became home. With Kim by my side, fraternity brothers nearby, and the excitement of the city around us, I felt grounded. At the same time, I never lost sight of the vision I had glimpsed in those sharply dressed sales reps. Retail was a stepping stone. I wanted independence, financial security, and a career that would challenge and reward me. That desire would push me toward the pharmaceutical industry, but in those early years, I was laying the foundation through hard work, friendships, and a growing family life in Los Angeles.

This was only the beginning of our little migration west. Each move felt like another step into the unknown, bringing new routines, discoveries, and challenges. Our first stop was Ardmore Street, just west of where we had been living before. The building itself felt like an upgrade. It had secured parking and sat in a better neighborhood, which gave us a sense of relief. Living in Los Angeles had already shown us how much difference one street could make. A place that seemed ordinary from the outside could mean a safer, quieter life inside, and Ardmore Street felt like that for us.

Before long, we packed up again and moved further west to Olympic Boulevard. This time we landed on the third floor of a large apartment building. From our window, the city stretched out in every direction, alive and constantly moving. By then Kim had already gone through a few different employment agencies. She was building her confidence, learning the ways of the city, and settling into her own rhythm.

I was starting to feel the same. After years of college and five years working at UCLA, I finally got the kind of opportunity I had been hoping for. Mobile Oil Company, a Fortune 500 company, offered me a position as a marketing representative. For me, this was more than a job. It meant stability, respect, and the start of a career. My role was to help independent business owners set up and operate gas stations. It might not have sounded glamorous, but to me it was a big deal.

When Mobile Oil hired me, they flew me back to Pennsylvania for training. That alone felt exciting. I had never been part of something so professional. The training included long hours in classrooms where we studied the business and time actually running a station myself. I learned the industry from the ground up, from stocking shelves to managing fuel sales. The idea was that once I returned to Los Angeles, I could train new station owners to do the same.

The timing was interesting. The service station business was in transition. Companies like Mobile were encouraging station owners to add retail stores inside their stations. Gas sales alone weren't enough anymore, but if customers came inside for snacks, groceries, or small household items, the profits could grow. I was being trained to carry that message west.

At the end of training, I was told I might eventually have to relocate out of California. That part hit me hard. Kim was finally getting settled, and the thought of uprooting her again didn't sit well. I loved the company, but California had started to feel like home, and I wanted to stay.

Life on Olympic Boulevard moved quickly. The street ran parallel to Wilshire, but during drive time it flowed much faster. Living in such a central spot gave us new experiences every day. Kim and I often had to pool our money when we wanted to eat out. There was a small Chinese restaurant we loved called The Dragon. The food was incredible, with portions big enough for leftovers. I remember one night counting pennies just to pay the bill, but it didn't matter. We were young, together, and The Dragon always made us feel welcome. None of the staff spoke much English, but they always seemed to understand us perfectly.

Some of our happiest moments then came when we just got in the car and drove. Cruising became our way of learning Los Angeles. The city was too big to figure out all at once, but each drive taught us a little more about its streets, neighborhoods, and character.

Kim needed to learn how to drive if we were going to get around. Los Angeles was built for cars. She went to driving school, taught by a man named Mr. Herman, who was patient but firm. She picked it up quickly.

Before Mobile Oil, I had worked at a recruiting firm, helping to place salespeople. From there I landed a job with Gallo Wine Company. That job gave me my first company car, a station wagon filled with sales materials and displays. My territory included many of the beach communities, which I never minded. On Fridays, I sometimes packed a change of clothes and cut out early to spend the afternoon at Venice Beach. That spot became my escape, a place to breathe and recharge.

One of our biggest adventures came when Kim and I decided to drive across the country. We had just bought our first new car, a Volvo 240 DL, straight off the lot. That car meant more than transportation. It was a symbol of progress. The trip took about two and a half days to get from California to Michigan, and then another full day to Ohio. The drive was long, but every mile felt worth it.

In Michigan, I saw my grandpa again. I'll never forget how proud he looked. It reminded me of where I had come from and how far I had gone. We also visited my mom and grandma, which filled me with comfort, before heading to Detroit to see Kim's family.

It was during that trip that Kim discovered she was pregnant. The news changed everything. Nine months later, our daughter, Shannon Nicole Smith, was born. The Volvo turned out to be the perfect car for that moment. Known as one of the safest cars on the road, it gave us peace of mind as new parents.

Shannon was born at Cedars-Sinai Hospital, just a short drive from our apartment on Olympic. After she arrived, our cruising adventures continued, but now we carried a diaper bag, bottles of formula, and a car seat in the back. Driving around with Shannon often became the easiest way to get her to sleep, and it worked every time.

Life changed in small ways. Breakfast outings now meant places like Denny's, where a crying baby wouldn't bother anyone. We adjusted quickly, learning how to be young parents in Los Angeles and enjoying life as best we could.

As Shannon grew, Kim and I realized we needed more space. We looked to Burbank, which sat just outside Los Angeles but felt like it was right next to Hollywood. The city carried its own magic, home to studios like Disney, Warner Brothers, and NBC, along with many record companies.

We found a new apartment complex near downtown Burbank. It was modern, lively, and filled with people connected to the entertainment industry. Many actors and actresses from soap operas lived there, and so did jazz musician Gerald Albright. I often ran into him in the elevator. He was one of the nicest people I had ever met, always polite and humble despite his talent. His wife, who managed his career at the time, kept him busy on the road for shows.

Even as we settled into Burbank, I never stopped searching for better opportunities. I checked the newspaper regularly, scanning for ads that might lead to something new. One day, I spotted a posting no bigger than half an inch for a pharmaceutical sales position. I figured it was worth a try and applied.

A week later, I got a call for an interview. I remember standing in a phone booth outside, sweating in the heat, while the interviewer asked me questions. The company turned out to be Allergan Pharmaceuticals, based in Orange County. They were interviewing candidates at the Marriott near LAX.

My first in-person interview was with the district manager, Robert Janisse. He was serious and sharp. He pulled out a sheet of paper and explained the flow of tears in the human eye, using technical language I could barely follow, then asked me to repeat it back. I stumbled through it and walked out convinced I had no chance.

To my surprise, they called me back for a second interview with the regional manager, Tom Mitro, a small but intense man. His questions were tough, though I can't recall the exact details now. What I do remember was the pressure and the seriousness of the process. A week later, Robert called me personally to offer me the job.

He explained I would go through a training program lasting a couple of months. It felt like the start of something completely new, and I was ready for it.

When Robert outlined what the job with Allergan would require, I felt both excited and terrified. Allergan made pharmaceuticals for the eye—steroids, antibiotics, beta blockers, and artificial tears. These were products eye doctors relied on, and now they would be my responsibility. Robert didn't sugarcoat it. The job demanded heavy training, and I needed to prepare myself.

I had to learn the physiology and anatomy of the eye, not just surface-level details. I needed to know product ingredients, how they worked, what conditions they treated, and how they compared to the competition. Doctors weren't going to take advice from someone who didn't know their stuff. Training meant two weeks away at a hotel, with exams that had to be passed. Failure meant dismissal.

The thought hit me hard. I smiled, but inside I was terrified. Science had never been my strength. In high school, I barely scraped by. Even in college, I avoided it. The only science-related course I took was oceanography, and I got a D. Now my career depended on mastering medical science.

Robert made sure I wouldn't face it unprepared. He paired me with a veteran sales rep, Bailey Crumpler, who handled major hospitals and teaching institutions. Bailey had seen it all and knew how to manage pressure. I shadowed him, studying his style and learning how to approach physicians.

There was also Kathy Lovejoy, sharp and confident, who had already proven herself in the field. I spent many days making sales calls with her, learning how to present, build trust, and navigate different personalities. Robert introduced me to a few others as well, each one adding something to my development. He wanted me to succeed and gave me the right mentors.

Finally, the time came for training. I packed my bags and headed to the hotel. In the classroom, there were about fourteen others from across the country. Our trainer, Steve Henderson, had once been a successful sales rep. He carried himself with confidence, and I later learned he had been a football player, which made sense. He had the presence of an athlete.

I noticed quickly that big companies liked athletes. They were competitive, resilient, and goal-oriented. If you had excelled in sports, it was worth mentioning in an interview because those qualities translated directly into sales. That realization stuck with me.

Training was no easy ride. We dove deep into eye physiology, drug formulations, and competitive products. We practiced presentations as if we were talking to doctors, explaining why our product was better and how it worked. Every morning we had tests on the previous day's lectures, and you needed an eighty-five percent to pass. The pressure was constant, but I managed to succeed each time. By graduation, I felt like I had survived boot camp.

Not long after, I attended my first sales meeting. Walking into that room was overwhelming. There were hundreds of people from across the country, including Ivy League graduates who were sharp and intimidating. I looked around and thought about how far I had come. I wasn't the smartest in the room, but I was holding my own.

Compensation was tied to performance, with salaries and bonuses based on territories. For the first time, I felt like I had arrived. No more dealing with retail frustrations. Now I was calling on physicians, and that felt like a huge step forward.

The structure of the job suited me. I worked from home with a company car. My days were spent seeing six to eight physicians, then finishing admin work back at the house. It gave me freedom but required discipline. No one was checking if I was awake. I had to get up, put on a suit, and go to work. The responsibility rested on me.

I stayed with Allergan for about five years. By the late 1980s, I was making good money and had become a bona fide pharmaceutical representative. I built up my wardrobe of suits, because sharp dress was expected in every office I visited. Over time, I learned to connect not only with physicians but with their staff. Nurses and receptionists often controlled access, and earning their trust gave me more opportunities. That one-on-one time became my strongest tool.

Meanwhile, Kim advanced in her own career at Disney. She worked as a recruiter, responsible for finding people to fill positions worldwide. Her attire shifted too, from silk dresses to business suits that reflected her growing role.

We began enjoying the rewards of our progress. I bought a white Mercedes 220, a clean four-door that turned heads. Kim looked beautiful driving it, and we both felt proud.

By 1997, a new chapter opened. I joined CibaVision Ophthalmics, a new division of Novartis. They built a powerhouse team by recruiting reps from Allergan, Merck, and Alcon. Leading the division was Daniel Myers, a man with the ability to move a room with his words.

At national sales meetings, Daniel always closed with motivational speeches. He had a way of making you want to run through a wall for him. I remember him saying, "I may not treat you equally, but I'll treat you fairly." That honesty earned respect.

He loved sports analogies. While he spoke, video clips played of Tiger Woods, Serena Williams, or John Elway, each one showing focus and determination. Daniel tied those images to our business, painting a picture that made you believe anything was possible.

One phrase stuck with me more than the rest: "What you do every day is not important, it's who you are that's critical." It reminded me the job was more than numbers. It was about character and how you carried yourself.

Back home, Kim teased me about the Mercedes, calling it "Luther" after Luther Vandross. Eventually, she wanted a change and moved on to a black Jaguar X-Type. By then, we already had three Volvos, and she was ready for something new. The Jaguar suited her perfectly.

We also started looking at houses. Our first home was in Sylmar, surrounded by mountains about forty minutes from Los Angeles. We had bought a small 1,500-square-foot house. On weekends, we sat outside and watched hang gliders leap from the top, gliding gracefully down to the park below. It became a ritual, sitting together, watching those colorful sails against the sky, and feeling grateful for where life had brought us.

I had just returned from a national sales meeting, and Kim was pregnant with our second child. When I walked in the door, she was already in full nesting mode—cleaning the house and getting everything ready for the baby's arrival.

That evening, things moved quickly. Unlike when Shannon was born, there wasn't a short drive to the hospital this time. We had to jump on the freeway and make our way into Los Angeles. Fortunately, traffic was flowing the other direction, leaving our side wide open for the drive to Cedars-Sinai.

The night itself felt strange. A lightning storm lit up the sky, adding an almost surreal backdrop to the trip. At the hospital, the halls were buzzing—it was a busy night for deliveries. Amid all the activity, our moment arrived, and soon after, Sydney Renée Smith was born.

Shannon now had a little sister.

Chapter 9:
Working At Ciba Vision

When I first started working with Ciba Vision Ophthalmics, I never imagined how quickly things would move or how creative I would need to be in order to stand out. The company had a solid line of ophthalmic products, and I was responsible for selling them across my territory. Among them was Voltaren, the very first nonsteroidal anti-inflammatory drop for eyes. It was a groundbreaking product, used primarily after surgery to reduce inflammation and pain.

At the time, Managed Care was having a huge impact on the way physicians could treat their patients. Insurance companies were dictating which drugs would be reimbursed, and if a medication was not covered, it was nearly impossible for doctors to prescribe it. One of the biggest players in California was Secure Horizons, a plan that covered an enormous number of seniors. Certain medical offices had the bulk of these patients, which meant those offices carried an incredible amount of influence. Every quarter, Secure Horizons would decide which new drugs to place on their formulary. If a drug made the list, physicians would write prescriptions for it because they knew their patients would be reimbursed. If it did not, then it was practically invisible.

I understood this system and knew I had to find a way to get Voltaren in front of the right people. That is when I came up with a strategy that ended up changing the trajectory of my career. I drafted three different versions of a letter that highlighted the advantages of prescribing Voltaren over competing products. The letters were clear, persuasive, and focused on why this new drug was the better choice for patients recovering from surgery.

Once I had my letters ready, I went to the physicians in my territory and asked them to read them. Many were impressed by the way the letters laid out the benefits, and with very little convincing, they agreed to sign them. After that, I would take the signed letters, put them on the doctor's own letterhead, and fax them directly from their offices to Secure Horizons. This made it look as though the request was coming straight from the physicians themselves.

I did this at several key offices, and by the time the P&T committee met to decide, Voltaren already had strong support. When the votes were counted, the decision to add Voltaren to the formulary passed with little resistance. Suddenly, Voltaren was the drug of choice for post-surgery care, and most physicians in my territory began prescribing it.

That breakthrough changed everything. I went from being a middle-of-the-pack representative to climbing quickly to number one in the country. It was a turning point in my career, and it showed me the power of thinking creatively in an industry that was often rigid and competitive.

Of course, Voltaren was not the only product I sold. Ciba Vision had a glaucoma drug called Betimol, which was another strong performer for me. Among the entire national sales force, I ranked seventh with Betimol, which was no small feat. I also had an allergy medication and an artificial tear product for dry eyes. With those, I ranked seventeenth and thirty-second in the country. By the end of the year, my performance across the board earned recognition.

The company honored me for being one of the top sales representatives in the country. But what stood out the most was when I received the NAGS Award, which stood for National Accounts Group. This was a direct result of my letter-writing idea, the one that gave Voltaren such a strong edge. For that award, they presented me with a heavy bust of a horse's head sculpture. I was told it was worth a lot of money, and while I could not say for sure what its market value was, it felt priceless because of what it represented.

Another recognition I received was the Tigers Award. This was given to the most aggressive sales representative in the company, and when they called my name, I could hardly believe it. The award itself was a sculpture of a tiger, bold and fierce, and it seemed to capture exactly how I had approached that year.

One of the biggest rewards came in the form of a trip. Kim and I were invited to attend President's Club in Maui, Hawaii. It was an all-expenses-paid week at the Grand Wailea Resort, one of the most beautiful places I had ever seen. It was an honor to be included, and it felt like a celebration of everything I had worked for.

The resort was stunning. They put us in a suite that had a huge balcony overlooking the ocean. At night, we could hear the waves crashing against the shore, a sound that was both powerful and soothing. During the day, the company rented us a Jeep so we could explore the island. We drove into little towns, wandered around, and soaked up the beauty of Maui.

The awards dinner in Maui was another highlight. That evening, Kim looked beautiful in her black gown as we walked into the ballroom. The company presented me with a plaque and a Ciba Vision ring, marking my achievements in front of my peers. It felt surreal. I remember thinking that the entire evening had a kind of dreamlike quality.

The trip had other memorable moments too. We saw Pierce Brosnan, who had taken on the role of James Bond after Sean Connery. We also crossed paths with Mike Tyson and his wife at the time. They were staying in a condo near the beach. Those celebrity sightings only added to the sense that the entire week was extraordinary.

We even attended a luau one night, a true Hawaiian tradition. The food, music, and dancing made it unforgettable. Kim and I soaked up every minute. When the trip ended, the company sent us home with gifts and mementos that filled our suitcases. It was one of those rare times in life that you know will stay with you forever.

Years later, I would hear about the tragic fire that devastated parts of Maui, including areas we had visited. It was heartbreaking to think about that beautiful island suffering such destruction. But my memories of that trip remained intact, untouched by the later tragedy.

In 1999, I was honored again with the same award. This time, the recognition included another trip to Hawaii, along with a Waterford Crystal piece as a parting gift. By then, I had grown used to the rhythm of the work, but being acknowledged never lost its meaning.

The feeling of being honored for hard work was familiar. It was the same kind of recognition I had felt when crossing the finish line, when the hours of training paid off, and when my name was called out for winning.

One year we had a national sales meeting in San Francisco, another city I had never been to. I had heard about it many times, but being there in person was different. The city reminded me a little bit of New York. It had the same feel of everything being close together, the tall buildings packed tight, the crowded streets, the fast pace of people rushing about their day. It was very different from Los Angeles. LA was so spread out that you had to drive everywhere, but San Francisco seemed to be stacked on top of itself, with hills that rose and dropped so steeply it felt like a ride each time you drove through the streets.

The bay caught my attention right away. It had a certain charm that Los Angeles never quite had. There was something more sophisticated about it, as if the air itself carried a touch of culture and history. In the mornings, a blanket of fog rolled in and hung low over the water, softening the edges of the city. Every so often you could catch a glimpse of the Golden Gate Bridge rising above the haze, a sight so iconic it almost didn't seem real.

We stayed at the Westin St. Francis Hotel, a place full of history and old-world class. I still remember being amazed when I found out they washed the coins at the front desk. Every time you got change it looked brand new, as if it had just been minted. The hotel carried a sense of dignity. You could almost feel the presence of the many famous people who had stayed there before. Presidents, queens, actors, even Theodore Roosevelt had walked through those doors. The place seemed untouched by time, proud of its tradition.

The staff made sure the atmosphere matched that level of grandeur. The valet stood tall in a long red coat with a black hat, ready to blow his whistle and summon a cab for guests. It felt like something out of a movie, the kind of treatment you did not see very often anymore. I remember one trip when Kim and I went there for an anniversary. I handed her a thousand dollars and told her to go shopping at Macy's. She lit up with excitement. The Macy's there had seven floors dedicated to women's clothes, while the men's store sat across the street. I wasn't in the mood to shop, so I went over to a Starbucks nearby and just people watched while she explored. Later that night, we had dinner together, sometimes at Morton's, other times down at Ghirardelli Square or close to Pier 39 at The Crab House.

San Francisco became a regular getaway for us. We often flew up on Friday evenings after work from Burbank Airport and spent the weekend there. By Sunday, we would head home, refreshed from the short trip. Kim loved shopping. She would beam with happiness just walking down the street, smiling at everything she saw. Kim would buy clothes and other things and ship them back home. It was one of her favorite places, and it quickly became one of mine too.

California was so large and full of variety that you could spend a lifetime exploring it. From Los Angeles to San Diego to San Francisco, and all the little towns and hubs in between, it was like several states wrapped into one. Each area had its own character, its own beauty.

In Southern California, my work with Ciba Vision covered the San Fernando Valley, which stretched from Glendale and Pasadena all the way north to Bakersfield. I also had the coastal areas, which included Ventura, Santa Barbara, and San Luis Obispo. Traveling that wide territory gave me a chance to see many sides of California.

San Luis Obispo was one of my favorite stops. It was bigger than Yellow Springs, where I grew up, but still small by Los Angeles standards. It was a green and quiet town, full of trees and open spaces. The people there were friendly, the doctors approachable and easy to talk to. I often stayed overnight when I went that far north because it took a couple of days to cover all my accounts. Thursdays were always my favorite days there because the downtown closed for the weekly farmers' market. The smell of barbecue filled the air while people bought food and sat on curbsides to eat. There was live music, a festive mood, and it made me feel like part of the community. I always tried to plan my visits for Thursdays so I could take it all in.

I often did office lunches for the staff and used the time to explain the benefits of my products to the doctors. My sales numbers from San Luis Obispo were always strong, and I credited the relationships I built there. Santa Barbara was another gem on my route. The town had a Spanish flair that made it stand out. I had excellent connections with the physicians there, and sometimes I arranged speaking engagements where I invited doctors from Los Angeles to come and talk about my products. These events cost a couple of thousand dollars, but they were always worth it because they helped grow my business.

Some of my best memories came from time spent with individual doctors. Dr. Stu Winthrop was one of them. His father had once owned a prestigious men's clothing store in Los Angeles called Dorman Winthrop. It was a landmark for more than four decades. Stu had inherited a sense of style, always dressing sharply, and he often complimented my ties. He told me I dressed well without trying to outshine the doctors, and I took that as a real compliment.

He once invited me to his home, which I should really call a castle. It sat high on a mountain with a view of Santa Barbara Bay. The scenery was breathtaking, something I'll never forget. Then there was Dr. Doug Katsev, a young surgeon in Santa Barbara at the time. He picked me up for lunch one day in a classic Volkswagen bug. We grabbed pizza from a local spot and went to his house, where we sat in his family room and ate. That was the kind of down-to-earth moment that built real friendships.

Ventura County, just south of Santa Barbara, was another part of my territory. It was not as stunning as Santa Barbara, but it was still a beautiful place. I had strong relationships with doctors there as well. Years later, a devastating fire swept through the coastal area and destroyed many homes. It was heartbreaking to see, but what struck me most was how quickly the community began to rebuild. That resilience was something I admired about California.

Farther north was Bakersfield, a dusty agricultural town in the middle of the state. It was a long drive, so I usually stayed overnight when I went there. It took a couple of days to see all the physicians in that area. The city itself wasn't glamorous, but the work was important, and I always tried to give my best effort no matter where I was.

Closer to home, I had Encino, Tarzana, Reseda, Northridge, Van Nuys, and Sherman Oaks, all part of the San Fernando Valley. Each city had its own personality, but together they formed the area I knew best. It was a busy and demanding territory, yet I was grateful for it. My work took me to so many different places, and in each one I found something memorable.

From the grandeur of San Francisco to the quiet charm of San Luis Obispo, from the Spanish streets of Santa Barbara to the resilience of Ventura, and even the dusty stretches of Bakersfield, I saw a California full of contrasts.

It was a state of endless possibilities, and I was lucky to experience so much of it while doing the work I loved.

The main street that ran through the Valley was Ventura Boulevard. If you grew up in Los Angeles, you could think of Ventura the same way you thought of Wilshire in the city. It stretched long and steady, connecting all the neighboring towns that shared the Valley. On that boulevard you could find everything, from small storefronts to towering buildings filled with doctors' offices and law firms. It had a rhythm of its own, always moving, always humming with a mix of business and life.

I remember one afternoon when I had an appointment with a doctor. His office always closed for lunch around the same time every day. A neat little sign was taped to the door saying they would reopen at two o'clock sharp. I was early, so I waited in the lobby. The building had a kiosk on the ground floor, and the security guard always sat there like it was his post. What made me laugh was what happened every lunch hour. The place would suddenly be full of women coming and going, dressed for work or just running errands, and the guard would nearly twist his neck off trying to greet each one. His head moved back and forth so quickly it was like he was watching a tennis match. He never missed a chance to say hello. As soon as lunch ended, the flood slowed to a trickle, and the building grew quiet again.

One particular day stands out. I was sitting there as usual, waiting for the time to pass, when a woman walked in. I couldn't see her face right away, but three guys trailed close behind, each of them snapping photo after photo. I heard the loud clicks echo through the lobby. She was slim, dressed simply, and wore oversized sunglasses. She stood at the directory board, checking the names of the offices and their suites while the cameras kept going. Finally, she turned in my direction. She pulled the glasses off, and in that moment I realized who she was. Halle Berry.

I just sat there thinking, "Damn, that's Halle Berry." Seeing celebrities on a screen or on the red carpet was one thing, but seeing them in real life was different. There were no stylists around, no perfect lighting, no designer gowns. They looked like regular people, just going about their business like anyone else.

I couldn't resist leaning over to the security guy after she left. I asked him, "Hey, did you see Halle Berry?" He nodded casually, like it was nothing. "Yeah," he said, "she comes here all the time." He told me she had a law office upstairs. To him it was routine. For me it was a little taste of how ordinary life in the Valley could brush up against Hollywood at any given moment. Another day in paradise, I thought.

Sometimes, when I wanted a break, I'd head over to Gelson's Market near Ventura and Havenhurst. They made some of the best sandwiches around, the kind that kept you coming back. That same store was where you could sometimes see the Jackson family. Their old compound was just off Ventura, and it wasn't unusual to hear that their mother still shopped there for groceries. My cousin had even married a CPA who lived in the neighborhood and managed money for professional athletes. Ventura Boulevard was full of stories like that.

If you headed east or south along the boulevard, you'd find yourself in Studio City. That part of town buzzed with production companies and studios. It wasn't unusual to walk into a deli there and find a famous face at the next table. Jerry's Famous Deli was one of my regular spots. The menu was huge, the kind of place you could go a dozen times and never order the same thing twice. I often went for lunch, sometimes alone, sometimes with a doctor I worked with.

One day I walked in and the place was quieter than usual. In the center of the room sat Pete Rose. He was just eating casually, talking to the owner of the deli, who stood next to him. It struck me how simple it all looked. No cameras, no crowds, just a man having lunch. That wasn't even the first time I'd seen him. Years later, when I heard Pete Rose had passed away on September 30, 2024, my mind went right back to that afternoon at Jerry's.

Not long after, my own career shifted. I interviewed for a new role within Ciba Vision, this time with the Retina Group. This wasn't the same as the larger sales force I had been part of. It was smaller, more elite, and the focus was on retina surgeons rather than general ophthalmologists. My territory changed too. I had all of Southern California now, stretching across Los Angeles County, down to San Diego, and even included trips to Las Vegas.

People assumed the Vegas trips meant nights at the casinos, but I had made a promise to myself. When I traveled for work, I wouldn't gamble. Those trips were strictly business. The routine became second nature. I would valet my car at the Burbank airport, walk across the street with my briefcase and an overnight bag, and board a short flight. When I landed in Vegas, a rental car was waiting. I could head straight to work without delay.

Retina specialists worked on the back of the eye, treating serious conditions like age-related macular degeneration and diabetic retinopathy. The drug I was selling then was called Visudyne. It wasn't like the usual eye drops most people imagined. Visudyne came as a green powder in a glass vial. It had to be reconstituted before being injected directly into the eye. The treatment didn't cure AMD, but it slowed its progression. Because of its cost, over a thousand dollars per unit, the sales numbers were significant, and so were the bonus checks.

One of the most influential doctors in my territory was Dr. David Boyer. He was well known, possibly one of the top retina specialists in the entire country. What made him stand out even more was his character. He was one of the kindest people you could hope to meet. Every year he hosted an office party at his home, and unlike most doctors, he invited a handful of sales reps. I was fortunate to be one of them.

One year, I even brought my daughter along. She ended up shooting pool by his swimming pool while I talked with him about work and life. His hospitality was genuine. At one point, he told me I could borrow his Mercedes sports car anytime. He joked that if I got a ticket, I'd have to pay for it myself. I never took him up on the offer. At the time, I drove a gray BMW 5 Series that was already fully loaded. I didn't feel the need to swap it out, but I always appreciated the gesture.

Dr. Boyer's practice had six other retina specialists, and together they purchased thousands of dollars' worth of Visudyne. That year, I ended up being the top salesperson in the country for Visudyne. At the national sales meeting, I was honored and celebrated. The reward was a President's Club trip, and that year it took us all the way to Nevis in the West Indies.

Nevis was a small island only thirty-two miles from the equator, but the company treated us like royalty. I cleared over a million dollars in sales that year, and the trip was designed to spoil us. We stayed at a Four Seasons resort, the kind of place where every detail was perfect. Kim went to the spa more than once. We had breakfast each morning by the pool, overlooking the suite. The days were slow, calm, and beautiful.

One day, they even flew us on a small plane to St. Martin. We spent time on both the French and the Dutch sides of the island. The people were welcoming everywhere we went, full of warmth and smiles. It was one of those experiences that stuck with me long after the trip was over.

Chapter 10:
From Oatmeal Mornings to Beverly Hills Nights

Every Friday morning, I made my way down to Torrance, a coastal city in the South Bay where the ocean air met the hum of early commuters. My destination was Dr. Ron Gallimore's retina practice, one of the busiest and most respected in the area. Visiting his office had become an important part of my routine, not just because of business but because I had grown to enjoy the rhythm of those mornings.

I always tried to get there before anyone else, usually just as the sun was starting to stretch across the streets. My first stop was the Starbucks a few blocks away. I would pick up a hot coffee and a cup of oatmeal, just the way Dr. Gallimore liked it. He loved oatmeal in the mornings, and I learned early on that the small gesture of bringing his breakfast went a long way. It showed respect, a kind of professional courtesy that helped build a good relationship. He appreciated it, and so did his staff.

By the time I arrived at the practice, the office wasn't officially open yet, but the team knew me well enough to buzz me in. The staff moved quietly through the halls, getting everything ready for the day. I'd step into his office, place the oatmeal and coffee neatly on his desk, and then settle onto his white leather couch with my iPad. It became my little workspace. I'd check my emails, catch up on reports, and sometimes review sales figures before the day officially started. The place always smelled faintly of disinfectant and fresh coffee, a mix that somehow felt comforting.

At some point, I would hear a faint knock at the back door. That was the signal that Dr. Gallimore had arrived. He was an early riser, the kind of person who didn't like wasting time. Most mornings, he had already been to the gym or out surfing before coming in. That was his way of clearing his mind before a long day of patient appointments. His energy was something I admired. He walked into his office with purpose, greeted his staff with a quiet smile, and slipped on his white lab coat like a man stepping into his second skin.

Before we'd exchange a word, his scribe would hand him the first chart of the day. He always started with his first patient before doing anything else. I respected that about him. He never let distractions take over, not even a business conversation. Once the first patient was seen, and the initial rush of the morning had settled, he'd make time for me. Sometimes we'd sit and talk about new treatments or products, sometimes just about life. His insights were sharp, his questions thoughtful, and even when he disagreed with something, he did it with respect. That was what made calling on his office a highlight of my week.

Over time, I had several offices in the South Bay that I visited regularly, but Dr. Gallimore's practice always stood out. There was something about the steady rhythm there, the balance between professionalism and warmth. I often told my kids that life had a funny way of surprising you, and I used to say, "Never say never, and never say forever." Change was the only constant, and I had learned that lesson many times in my career. Just when things seemed settled, something new would always come along.

That truth became real once again when our parent company, Novartis, went through a major management shake-up. The shift hit every part of the business, including the Retina Group. Suddenly, the entire sales force was being called to East Hanover, New Jersey, for another round of corporate training. It felt like déjà vu. We had already been through the same kind of training when the company first launched its retina products, and now here we were, packing our bags again.

The timing couldn't have been more inconvenient. It was about a week before Thanksgiving, and the weather back east was bitterly cold. I remember thinking about those frosty New Jersey mornings as I looked out at the California coastline during my last few calls before the trip. The South Bay breeze felt almost like a luxury I was about to leave behind. Still, I knew how these things worked. When management changed, so did everything else. New people at the top wanted to understand what they were inheriting, and that meant we had to start from square one.

It wasn't just our group. The entire sales division across the country was being brought in. It was a massive undertaking, a mix of familiar faces and new ones all converging in one place to go over the same material we had already mastered. It felt redundant in some ways, but it was also a reminder that business runs on structure. Even when you know the ropes, someone always wants to make sure you're holding them the right way.

When I arrived in East Hanover, the cold hit me hard. The skies were gray, and the air smelled like rain and asphalt. The training campus was sprawling, a mix of modern offices and glass conference rooms filled with energy and chatter. Everyone was bundled up, clutching their coffee cups, swapping stories about their flights and how early they had to leave home. There was a kind of shared fatigue in the air, but also a strange excitement. A management shake-up always brought uncertainty, but it also created opportunity. You never really knew what direction things might take next.

Inside the training rooms, everything was as polished as ever. The presentations, the branding, the motivational speeches, they all had that corporate shine. We went through slides about products we had been selling for years, discussing strategies we already knew by heart. Some people took notes like it was all new, while others just nodded politely, waiting for the next session to start. It was a strange mix of repetition and routine, but I reminded myself that this was part of the job. Change was uncomfortable, but it was necessary.

In between sessions, I found myself thinking back to those quiet mornings in Torrance. The steady hum of the office, the smell of oatmeal and coffee, and the way Dr. Gallimore greeted the day with calm focus. Compared to the constant buzz of the corporate world, his practice felt like another universe. Out there, every decision was measured, every move deliberate. Here, everything moved fast, decisions shifted daily, and stability was an illusion.

Still, there was something grounding about being back with the whole team. We were all in the same boat, navigating whatever changes came next. There were moments of laughter in the hotel lobby, long dinners where we talked about our families and shared old stories from the field. For a few days, the cold didn't feel so harsh. It was a reminder that behind every sales figure and corporate meeting were people just trying to do their best.

When the training sessions ended and we prepared to head home, I packed my bag with a strange mix of exhaustion and anticipation. The company was changing, the leadership was new, and none of us really knew what the next chapter would look like. But that was the thing about this business, you learned to adapt. I thought of the words I often told my kids again: never say never, never say forever.

Because at work, just like in life, everything keeps moving.

When I think back to that trip to New York, I can still feel the chill in the air. It was my first weekend there, about a year after 9/11, and the city still carried a heaviness that was hard to describe. I stayed at the Marriott Hotel, just around the corner from Ground Zero. Even though the area was full of construction noise and the constant movement of people trying to rebuild, there was a strange quietness that lingered in the streets at night. It was winter, and for someone used to California weather, the biting cold made every walk outside a small battle. I remember pulling my coat tighter and thinking how much I missed the warm, dry air of home.

During that trip, though, something unexpected caught my attention. There was a conversation I overheard one evening about a new company starting up called Eyeonics. The name stuck in my head. Maybe it was the sound of it, or maybe it was because I was always curious about anything connected to the medical field. When I got back to my hotel room that night, I opened my laptop and started searching. The company was based in Orange County and was in the process of building a salesforce. That immediately sparked my interest.

Not long after that, I got a phone call from a man named Greg Sanchez. He introduced himself as a Regional Director for Eyeonics. I remember I was on a short break between meetings when he called, so I stepped into the hallway to hear him better. He had an easygoing but confident tone. Greg told me they were building a new sales team from the ground up and were looking for people with experience in medical sales. My heart jumped a little at that. The idea of joining a startup in such an innovative field sounded exciting. I told him I would love to meet and learn more about what they were doing.

We agreed to meet in two weeks, right after I got back from my trip to New Jersey. As soon as I hung up, I knew what I had to do next: my homework. I spent every evening after work researching everything I could about Eyeonics. From what I learned, they specialized in making lens implants for the eye. That caught my attention because I knew how significant cataract surgery was for millions of people every year.

Cataracts, as I understood, happen when the natural lens of the eye, called the crystalline lens, becomes cloudy with age. When you're young, that lens is crystal clear and flexible, bending easily to focus on near and distant objects. But as the years pass, it hardens and starts to yellow, slowly blurring your vision. The standard procedure for decades had been to remove that old lens and replace it with a fixed artificial one. The problem was that once you had the surgery, you still needed glasses for either near or distance vision.

What Eyeonics was developing changed that. Their implant was designed to act just like the eye's natural lens. It could shift focus, flex, and adjust, giving people back the ability to see clearly at multiple distances without glasses. That was revolutionary. I realized right then that this wasn't just another medical product, it was something that could change lives. And I wanted to be part of that.

By the time I met Greg Sanchez two weeks later at another Marriott Hotel, this one in California, I was ready. I came prepared with a full business plan I had put together myself. It detailed how I would approach the top ophthalmologists in Los Angeles, how I would introduce them to the product, and how I planned to build relationships that would lead to strong adoption. I even made a list of every major surgeon in my territory, complete with notes on their background and practice style. I wanted Greg to see that I was not just interested. I was committed.

Greg was polite and professional during our meeting. He listened carefully as I presented my plan. We talked about the challenges of entering a competitive market, about surgeons' skepticism when faced with new technology, and about the strategies needed to overcome those hurdles. I left that meeting feeling confident.

A week later, though, I got the news that Greg had chosen someone else for the position. It hit me harder than I expected. I had put my best effort into preparing for that opportunity, and hearing that it went to someone else felt like the air had gone out of me. I tried not to take it personally, but it was hard not to.

I decided I would return to Novartis, where I had been working as a senior sales representative. It was familiar, stable, and a place where I was respected. Still, something about Eyeonics lingered in my mind. I kept thinking about their vision and the kind of people they were likely hiring: pioneers, risk-takers, people willing to bet on innovation.

Then, about a month later, the phone rang again. It was Greg Sanchez. I remember I was at my desk when I saw his name appear on my phone. He sounded upbeat. He told me there was a new opening for a representative to cover the Los Angeles North territory. I could feel my excitement building as he spoke.

Greg said I didn't need to go through another interview with him. Instead, he wanted me to meet in Orange County, in Aliso Viejo, with the man who would be my direct supervisor and also with the CEO of the company. It was going to be a more formal introduction to the leadership team. I thanked him and agreed right away.

I didn't know it then, but that next meeting would change the course of my life. I spent the next several days preparing again, revisiting my notes and updating my business plan. I wanted to understand every technical detail of the product so that I could speak confidently about it. I practiced my pitch, rehearsed answers to potential questions, and even researched the executives I was about to meet.

On the day of the meeting, I drove to Aliso Viejo early, the morning air filled with that mix of nerves and hope that comes before something important. The company's building stood on a quiet street lined with palm trees, a reminder that I was back on my home turf in Southern California. As I walked into the lobby, I took a deep breath and reminded myself that no matter what happened, I was ready.

The receptionist greeted me and offered me a seat while she let them know I had arrived. I sat there, glancing at the company's logo on the wall and thinking about how quickly things had turned around. A few weeks earlier, I had thought that door had closed. Now it was wide open again.

When Greg walked in, he smiled and shook my hand firmly. He introduced me to the man who would soon become my boss and to the CEO, who had a calm but commanding presence. They both spoke passionately about the company's mission and their belief that their lens could transform the way cataract surgery was done. Listening to them, I felt something shift inside me. It wasn't just a job anymore, it felt like the beginning of something bigger.

As we talked about the product, the market, and the future, I realized how much I wanted to be part of this. I could see the potential, not only in the technology but in the people leading it. I left that meeting with my mind racing and my heart full of anticipation, not yet knowing how deeply this opportunity would shape the next chapter of my career and my life.

When I arrived at Eyeonics that morning, I had no idea how much that day would shape the next few years of my life. The building was almost empty, its hallways quiet, the kind of quiet that comes when a company is still finding its feet. I was told I'd be meeting my immediate boss first, a man named Craig Measel.

When he walked in, I immediately noticed his tall frame, about six feet two, with short, neat hair and an easy smile. He wore a Tommy Bahama shirt and casual slacks, looking more like someone on vacation than a corporate manager. I thought to myself, *he looks like a big Ken doll.* He extended his hand, and his grip was firm but friendly. We hit it off right away, and after a few minutes of small talk, he told me I was about to meet the vice president of the company, a man named Ron Goldrich who had flown in from Florida.

Ron came in wearing, you guessed it, another Tommy Bahama shirt. It was clear this was the unofficial company uniform. He had an upbeat energy that filled the room. The three of us walked into a small conference room, the walls still bare, the faint smell of new paint lingering in the air. Ron sat across from me, glanced at my résumé, and said, "I've already looked over your background. I know all about you. I've got just one question. Do you want the job?"

I was caught off guard by his directness. Before I could answer, he turned to Craig and asked, "What do we expect this territory to bring in the first year?"

Craig replied without hesitation, "Seven hundred fifty thousand dollars would be the quota."

Ron nodded, then looked back at me. "We'll start you at a base salary of a hundred thousand a year plus commission. You'll earn seven percent of everything you sell."

I smiled and said, "I think I'll hang out with you guys for a while." That got a laugh out of both of them.

Ron leaned back in his chair and said, "The most important thing now is that you meet Andy Corley, our CEO. He's the one you need to close. Close him hard for the job."

They explained the training process to me. I'd be responsible for instructing doctors on how to perform the lens implant surgeries. To start, I would need to complete a preceptorship, spend a week shadowing a doctor in his practice and in the operating room. I listened closely, my mind already racing ahead to what this job could become.

Then the moment came. Andy Corley entered the room. He had short gray hair, kind eyes, and the same casual look as the others. He carried himself with the quiet confidence of someone used to being in charge. I introduced myself and began describing my background, emphasizing my knowledge of the territory and how well I knew the doctors and their practices. I made it clear how badly I wanted the position and how determined I was to grow this market. Finally, I asked, "So when do I start?"

Andy smiled. "Ron will give you your start date. Welcome to the team."

The next thing I knew, we were all heading to lunch together. Andy offered to drive, and we climbed into his big black Mercedes S-Class. It fit him perfectly: refined, strong, and understated. I sat in the back seat, listening to them talk, feeling a mix of excitement and disbelief. I had just landed one of the best opportunities of my career.

At lunch, the conversation shifted from business to the science behind the product. Andy explained the concept of the Crystalens implant and how it allowed patients to see clearly at multiple distances without glasses. He told me how doctors could offer it as a premium upgrade to patients, improving both outcomes and profitability. The catch was that surgeons had to take a specialized course and become certified to perform the procedure.

He also told me about the American Academy of Ophthalmology conference, the AAO, held every year. It was a huge event that brought together eye surgeons from all over the world to discuss innovations and new technology. Eyeonics would be there, showcasing the lens and hosting training sessions.

Over the next two months, I focused on getting doctors enrolled in those certification courses. It was the key to our success. By the end of that period, I had nearly thirty surgeons signed up, one of the highest numbers in the company. At one of our local meetings, they even called my name and recognized me for it. It felt good to be part of something growing so fast.

As part of my perceptorship, I worked with Dr. Michael Colvard, one of the top ophthalmologists in my territory. His office was in Van Nuys, a busy practice with patients coming and going all day. During that week, I watched him perform about eight Crystalens implants. I studied every movement of his hands, every decision he made during surgery. Each time, I saw the precision and confidence that only years of experience could build.

The next day, when patients came back for their follow-up visits, many of them could already see 20/20 and read without glasses. Their smiles said everything. I remember thinking how incredible it was to witness that kind of transformation. Some patients would look at me and thank me as if I had done the surgery myself. I'd quickly explain that it was Dr. Colvard who deserved the credit. I was just the guy who provided the lens.

Still, those moments made me proud. I believed in the product and in the company. I worked hard, built relationships, and made sure my surgeons had everything they needed to succeed. Within my first year, I became one of the top three representatives in the entire country. My quota fell just short, but I still made nearly a hundred seventy thousand dollars that year.

I decided to treat myself and bought a navy blue Range Rover, the kind of car that made every drive feel like an event. I enrolled my youngest daughter in tennis lessons, and she loved it. She would beam with excitement each time we pulled up to a match, her tennis racket bouncing on her shoulder as she hopped out of the SUV.

Kim and I also took a big step. We had a five-bedroom house built just north of Los Angeles, tucked away in a quiet suburb. It was the kind of home we had dreamed of for years, a place big enough for the kids to grow, with a backyard that caught the soft California sunsets.

My second year was even better. I earned over two hundred thousand dollars and had built strong relationships with surgeons throughout my territory. I made sure to take my doctors to some of the best restaurants in Los Angeles. We went to Spago, Katsuya, and BOA Steakhouse; if it was on the city's hot list, I had probably dined there. Those dinners weren't just about food; they were about trust, connection, and partnership.

Each time I drove home after a long day or a late dinner meeting, I felt a deep sense of satisfaction. Not because of the paycheck or the car or even the title, but because I knew I was part of something that mattered.

Eyeonics was still new, but it was growing fast, and so was I.

I remember one evening when I first walked into CUT, Wolfgang Puck's famous restaurant in Beverly Hills. The place had an air of sophistication that hit you the moment you stepped through the doors. The lighting was soft but golden, and everything gleamed. You could tell it was the kind of restaurant where people came to be seen. I had heard plenty about it, but being there in person felt like stepping into a different world.

As I was settling into my table, something unexpected happened. Lionel Richie walked right by. I looked up, half in disbelief, and before I could even react, he caught my eye, smiled, and reached out his hand. He shook mine like we were old friends and asked how I was doing. I had never met him before in my life, yet his warmth made it feel natural, easy. For a second, I forgot I was in one of the most exclusive restaurants in Beverly Hills. I just sat there grinning, thinking how surreal it was to have Lionel Richie casually greet me at dinner.

The place had that kind of energy. You never knew who might walk by or sit at the table next to you. It was a world that felt both distant and familiar at the same time.

On another night, I went to the bar across the hallway from CUT. It was late, and the place had that quiet hum that comes after the dinner rush. I ordered a drink and leaned back, people-watching. A few minutes later, I noticed someone who looked strikingly familiar standing at the far end of the bar. I blinked twice before realizing who it was: Jason Statham, the star from *The Transporter*. He looked exactly as he did on screen, calm, confident, a little mysterious. Nobody bothered him, which somehow made the whole thing even cooler. Beverly Hills was full of moments like that.

CUT itself was unlike any restaurant I had ever been to. The décor was striking and almost intimidating in its simplicity. The walls were lined with huge black-and-white photographs of famous faces, celebrities, athletes, and politicians. They were all captured from the chest up, their faces perfectly still, eyes serious, not a hint of a smile. Arnold Schwarzenegger's photo hung there, along with Brad Pitt's, Prince's, and even President Obama's. None of the photos were labeled, so half the fun was figuring out who was who.

Even the menus were a surprise. Each one had a different celebrity face printed on the back, again without names. When the waiter handed them out, everyone at the table would flip theirs over to see who they got. It became a little game at every dinner. Someone would say, "Who do you have?" and you'd see everyone turning their menus over, laughing, guessing, debating. It was a small touch, but it gave the place personality, something that made it stand out from every other fine dining spot in the city.

I used to take my doctors to CUT sometimes after appointments or when we needed to discuss something important outside the hospital. It was the kind of place that made everyone sit up straighter, speak a little softer, and enjoy themselves just a bit more. After those dinners, I would find myself going back the next weekend with Kim. We both loved the food, but I think we loved the atmosphere even more. There was always something to look at, someone to notice, a conversation that started because of the strange quiet intensity of those expressionless faces staring down from the walls.

Thinking back on those days, it's funny how much things have changed. There was a time when we couldn't get a table anywhere because we didn't have reservations. We would drive around for what felt like hours, going from one restaurant to the next, hoping someone had a cancellation. We'd laugh about it, trying to make the best of it, but it was frustrating, too. That all changed later. Eventually, getting into places like CUT wasn't a problem anymore. I could call ahead or just walk in, and there would always be a table waiting.

I even remember when my mom came to visit. She and my mother-in-law were both in town, and I wanted to treat them to something special. I didn't take them to CUT, though. For them, I chose Spago, another one of Wolfgang Puck's restaurants, a place with a lighter, more relaxed atmosphere for lunch. Watching the two of them sitting there, talking and laughing, made me realize how different things had become. My mom wasn't used to places like that, but she enjoyed every second. She kept looking around, soaking it all in, as if she couldn't quite believe where she was. When I took my mother-in-law, on the other hand, fit right in. She chatted easily with the staff, complimented the food, and even managed to get a few laughs out of our waiter.

The little things stood out to me the most. I didn't have to circle the block for parking anymore, worrying about feeding a meter or finding a spot in some dark alleyway. Now I could pull right up to the entrance, hand over my keys, and let the valet take care of it. It sounds small, but in Los Angeles, that was luxury. I'd step out of the car, straighten my jacket, and walk inside without a second thought.

Those evenings always had a certain rhythm. The clinking of glasses, the low hum of conversation, the soft light bouncing off the polished tables. The waiters moved like clockwork, always appearing at the right time without ever feeling intrusive. Every plate that came out looked like it belonged in a magazine. The food was rich, perfectly cooked, every bite layered with flavor.

I'd glance around sometimes and catch sight of people I recognized from television or the news. They were always there, scattered among the regular diners, blending in yet standing out. The funny thing about CUT was that even though it was full of famous people, it never felt pretentious. It was elegant, yes, but not overbearing. The staff treated everyone the same, whether you were a movie star or someone just celebrating a birthday.

I remember the first time I brought Kim there, how her eyes lit up when she walked through the doors. She loved everything about the place, the sleek design, the photographs, the little guessing game with the menus. We'd sit there for hours, taking it all in, talking about work, family, or whatever came to mind. Sometimes we'd plan to leave early, but somehow dessert would appear, and another hour would pass before we realized how late it had gotten.

There was something grounding about those nights. In a city built on appearances, CUT managed to make everything feel authentic. Maybe it was the food, maybe the people, or maybe just the feeling of being part of something special, even for a few hours.

Whenever I think of those times, I can almost hear the soft chatter, smell the food coming from the kitchen, and feel that slight buzz of excitement in the air. I can picture Lionel Richie smiling as he shook my hand, Jason Statham standing quietly at the bar, and the faces on those walls watching over everyone without saying a word. It was a world that moved fast, but for a few moments inside that restaurant, time seemed to slow down just enough for me to take it all in.

Chapter 11:
The CEO Ride-Along

When I first learned that Andy Cooley, our CEO, would be spending a day with me in the field, I knew it was one of those moments that could either make or break a career. It was customary for him to ride along with certain sales reps from time to time. Sometimes he visited those who were leading in sales, and other times he spent the day with the ones who were struggling. Either way, the idea was simple. He wanted to see what was really happening in the field, to understand the rhythm of our days, and to hear directly from the doctors we worked with.

I had always prided myself on running a solid territory, so I wasn't nervous. Still, there's something about having the CEO sitting next to you that keeps you on your toes. Andy wasn't the kind of leader who hid behind emails or corporate meetings. He liked to see things for himself. He wanted to watch interactions, listen to what the surgeons said, and get a sense of how the business looked at the ground level. That was exactly what this day was about.

By then, I was driving a sleek black Porsche Cayenne S. I took a bit of pride in that car. It wasn't just a vehicle; it was a statement of the work I had put in and the success I'd earned. Andy climbed into the passenger seat that morning, dressed sharp as ever. He wore a dark sports coat over a crisp white shirt, open at the collar with no tie, and his cell phone in hand. That phone was his whole office. While some managers still carried notebooks and planners, Andy typed everything into his phone. Notes, numbers, reminders, it was all in there.

"Morning," he said in that easy Southern drawl of his. I always suspected he was from Georgia. The accent gave him a relaxed charm that made people want to talk to him, even when they were nervous.

He settled into the seat and looked around the car with a quick grin. "Nice ride," he said.

"Thanks," I replied, starting the engine.

"So," he asked as we pulled out of the parking lot, "how's your territory? Any fires to put out? Any surprises?"

I had prepared for that question. I always did. Whenever a manager or executive came into the field, I made sure to have a full summary ready to hand them. That morning, I had a two-page document sitting neatly in the center console. It outlined every doctor we would visit, notes on their practices, any recent surgeries they'd performed with our implants, and follow-up results. It also included my sales numbers, pipeline opportunities, and challenges I was addressing.

"Here's the lay of the land," I said, handing it over.

He glanced at it, scrolling through the pages with his thumb. "You're thorough," he said. "I like that."

Most reps, especially the newer ones, never bothered to go that far. They'd show up with nothing more than an itinerary or a list of names scribbled on a notepad. That might have worked for some, but not for me. I wanted anyone who rode with me to know that I understood every detail of my business. It wasn't just about sales numbers; it was about relationships. Every surgeon, every nurse, every operating room staff member had a story, and I made sure to know it.

Andy had a reputation that made a lot of people nervous. Everyone in the company had heard the stories. If he rode with you and didn't like what he saw, that could be your last day. There were no second chances when it came to poor performance. I had no intention of becoming one of those stories.

Our first stop that morning was a large surgical center downtown. The surgeon we were visiting was one of the best in the region, known for his precision and steady hands. As we walked in, the nurses greeted me by name, smiling as they saw I had company. Andy hung back slightly, watching everything. I could tell he was assessing not just the doctor's feedback but also how I interacted with everyone around me.

The meeting went smoothly. The surgeon had only good things to say about the implants and how well his patients were doing. He even complimented our service response times and the quality of our follow-ups. That kind of feedback was music to any CEO's ears, and I could see the satisfaction on Andy's face.

From there, the day was a blur of hospitals, clinics, and surgeries. We split our time strategically. Andy attended a few of the procedures himself, observing the surgeons in action, while I went across town to handle other cases. By noon, we had covered half the city. Each stop reinforced the same message: our products were working, and our relationships were strong.

At one point, while driving between cases, Andy looked over and said, "You seem to really know your surgeons. That's not something you can fake."

I smiled. "It's taken time. You learn who they are, what they like, and how they work. Some want data, others want reassurance. You give them what they need to do their job better."

He nodded thoughtfully, typing something into his phone. I couldn't tell if it was a note or just him checking his messages, but it didn't matter. I knew I was doing exactly what I was supposed to.

The afternoon moved fast. At each stop, the pattern repeated itself. Doctors were satisfied, patients were seeing great outcomes, and the feedback was positive. By the time we finished our last visit, we had a list of successful cases that spoke for themselves. The results from recent surgeries were coming in, and many patients were reporting 20/20 vision and clear reading ability without glasses. Those were the numbers that mattered.

As we sat in traffic on the way back, the sun dipping low on the horizon, Andy leaned back in his seat and said, "You're running a tight ship out here. I like that."

I appreciated the compliment, though I didn't say much. It felt good to know my hard work was being recognized.

When I dropped him off at his hotel later that evening, he shook my hand firmly. "Keep doing what you're doing," he said. "That's how you build a career."

I watched him walk inside, still sharp in that same white shirt, still holding that ever-present phone. Then I sat in my car for a few moments, letting the day sink in.

The next morning, I was back in the field. The pace never slowed. It was always about the next case, the next follow-up, the next patient. But there was a quiet satisfaction that came with knowing the CEO had seen the work firsthand. The outcomes spoke louder than any report ever could.

When those patients came back with clear vision, able to see both distance and small print without glasses, it meant everything. It wasn't just about the commission checks, though those months could be good ones, fifteen to twenty thousand dollars sometimes. It was about being part of something that worked.

Andy's visit had reminded me that preparation, consistency, and genuine care made all the difference. And that day, driving my black Cayenne from one hospital to the next, I knew exactly why I loved what I did.

Craig Measel was the kind of boss people remembered for all the right reasons. He had a sharp marketing mind and was always thinking up new ideas to keep our work exciting. He had this habit of saying, "Michael, let me show you something new I'm working on. What do you think of this?" and every time, it felt like he was inviting me to be part of something that mattered. After every ride-along or field visit, he'd wrap things up by telling me I was doing a great job. He didn't just manage; he inspired. That, I learned, was what made him so effective. He was quick to troubleshoot when things went wrong and never shied away from challenges.

Of course, not everything ran smoothly. We had our share of problems. Sometimes an implant would go in upside down, or a lens would turn out to be warped or have the wrong power. There was also something called Z Syndrome. That happened when the lens wasn't seated properly inside the capsule or if the bag was too tight, causing the lens to bend in a Z shape once inside the eye. Surgeons didn't like mistakes, and the operating room was not the place to make one. We always tried to get it right the first time, because you never wanted to be the reason a case didn't go as planned.

My job was to convince doctors to use our implant, the Crystalens, and I had a knack for it. Once a surgeon saw how smooth the surgery could go and how good the results were, they became loyal customers. But the real hook came when they realized how much extra money they could earn from offering the lens as a premium option. Regular implants didn't bring in much profit, but Crystalens was different. It gave patients better vision and gave doctors an incentive to recommend it. Once they saw that, they were sold.

I remember a big presentation I gave in West Hollywood to Dr. Arthur Benjamin. He had a huge Russian patient base and a staff that spoke the language fluently. His practice was busy, but he wasn't completely convinced about Crystalens yet. I came prepared with studies that showed how well the lens performed. Afterward, he invited me out back for a cigarette. It became something of a routine. He'd smoke, and we'd talk about upcoming cases and which patients he wanted to try the lens on. Before long, he became one of our strongest supporters. He liked the lens, liked the results, and liked the extra income it brought in.

There were moments when I'd stop and take it all in. I was working in Beverly Hills, West Hollywood, and downtown Los Angeles, places where you could feel the pulse of success and fame in the air. I often thought about how lucky I was to be right in the middle of it all. One afternoon, I was leaving a building in Beverly Hills when I saw Sugar Ray Leonard standing there in sweatpants, talking on his phone. He gave me a nod as I passed by. I quietly said his name under my breath, not wanting to interrupt his call, but just to mark the moment. "Sugar," I whispered, smiling to myself.

Not every day was spent among the stars. Some days started long before sunrise. When I had cases up in Santa

Barbara with Dr. Stewart Winthrop, I'd be on the road by four in the morning. I always took the back route, winding through the hills as the sky slowly turned from black to blue. There was something peaceful about those drives. The air felt fresher, and the scenery looked like a painting with rolling fields, the ocean in the distance, and the sun rising behind the hills.

Once I got to Santa Barbara, I had a ritual. I'd stop for breakfast at a little place called The Cajun Kitchen. They made the best red snapper with scrambled eggs and hash browns. I'd sit outside on the porch with my coffee and watch the town come to life. When breakfast was done, I'd head over to the surgery center and help the nurses get ready for Dr. Winthrop's cases. He usually had eight surgeries that morning, and three of them were Crystalens implants. I'd make sure everything was set up perfectly, that the lenses were ready, and the nurses knew exactly how to load them.

After the cases, Dr. Winthrop and I would usually grab lunch downtown before I headed back to Los Angeles. Those days were long, but I didn't mind. There was something rewarding about being part of a good team and seeing patients come out of surgery with better vision.

Another surgeon I worked closely with was Dr. John Davidson in Ventura County. John was one of the most well-read people I knew. He didn't just read medical journals; he read everything, like books about cars, technology, and whatever caught his attention. He was tall, probably over six feet, and one of the most skilled surgeons in the business.

His movements in the operating room were fast but never rushed. Everything he did was precise.

One thing that always stood out about John was how high he kept his surgical table. Most doctors positioned it lower, but he preferred it raised. He said it helped take pressure off his back, and after years of bending over patients, he had learned what worked best for him.

Outside the hospital, John had another side to him. He was a jazz musician and played bass in a local band. One night, I drove up to Santa Barbara just to watch him perform. He was good, too. During surgeries, he'd often have jazz playing from his iPhone through the operating room speakers, setting a calm rhythm for everyone to work to.

That night, after his show, I helped him carry his gear out to his car. He drove a black Mercedes station wagon that was anything but ordinary. It had two iPod hookups, a killer sound system, and fat 22-inch rims that gleamed under the parking lot lights. It looked fast even when it was parked. I remember thinking how much that car fit him—elegant, smooth, and powerful without being flashy.

Cars had always fascinated me. California only deepened that love. You could see every kind here, from classic Mustangs and restored Camaros to sleek European sports cars that looked like they belonged in magazines. Sometimes, driving up the coast, I'd catch myself daydreaming about owning one of those someday. It wasn't just about the car. It was the feeling of freedom, the idea that you could take off down the Pacific Coast Highway with the windows down and the whole world stretched out in front of you.

Those were the days when work didn't feel like work. I was learning, growing, and meeting people who were the best at what they did. Every doctor had a different personality, a different way of approaching surgery, and I adapted to each one. Some liked to talk through every detail, others preferred silence, and a few wanted to joke around before the first incision. It kept things interesting.

Whether it was Craig with his new marketing ideas, Dr. Benjamin with his Russian patients, or Dr. Davidson with his jazz and fast cars, every person I met left an impression on me.

I remember one afternoon driving back from the Lancaster and Palmdale area, two quiet desert towns about forty-five minutes north of where I lived. I had been up there for business with one of my surgeons and was heading home. The day had gone well, and I felt like I was on top of the world.

Before I started the drive, I noticed a leftover joint sitting in the ashtray. My car at the time was a black Audi S5 with a V8 engine. I'll never forget that car. My daughter's bedroom sat right above the garage, and she used to joke that the Audi sounded like the space shuttle whenever I pulled in. That engine had a deep growl that made the walls vibrate.

The freeway I was on was called the 14. In the middle of the afternoon, there were hardly any cars on the road. I loosened my tie, tossed my suit jacket on the passenger seat, and turned the music up. The volume filled the cabin as I sped along, the dry wind rushing in through the window. I had just closed a big deal and was feeling good, really good.

Before long, I looked down and realized I was flying, must have been going at least 130 miles per hour. In California, that kind of speed can land you straight in jail. As I passed a California Highway Patrol car parked on the shoulder, my heart sank. I knew I was in trouble.

Immediately, I slowed down and rolled down all the windows, hoping to clear out the smell of cannabis before the officer reached me. I pulled over before they even had the chance to turn on their lights. Sure enough, the CHP car came speeding up behind me, lights flashing.

When the door opened, out stepped not the kind of officer I expected. She was short, older, wearing glasses, and moved carefully toward me with one hand resting on her sidearm. I rolled down my window and said, "Ma'am, I'm sorry. I know I was speeding." I already had my license and registration ready for her.

She looked a little nervous, like she didn't quite trust the situation yet. She finally said, "You were going really fast. You know the ticket for that could be serious."

I nodded, completely honest. "I know, ma'am. I deserve the ticket."

After a long pause, she scribbled something on her pad and handed it over. To my surprise, the ticket only said I was doing eighty-five. I couldn't believe it. I had just been saved from what could have been a much worse day. I thanked her and promised to slow down.

Later, I took an online traffic school course so the ticket wouldn't raise my insurance rates. Kim, my wife, used to tell me I needed to "shake that car." She said it half-jokingly, but I knew what she meant. Maybe she worried I'd wreck it one day, or maybe she just thought the thirteen-hundred-dollar monthly payment was crazy. Either way, she was right about one thing: I was living fast.

At the time, I was a medical device account representative, pulling in fifteen to twenty thousand a month in commissions. When you make that kind of money, it's easy to feel invincible. Kim was doing well, too. She worked at Disney and looked like she belonged in a magazine spread, walking into work in designer suits and heels from Louboutin or Jimmy Choo. She had her own goals, and we both liked the good life.

After a while, I started worrying about my Range Rover. It was racking up miles, and I knew repairs would start piling up soon. One rainy day in Los Angeles, I stopped by the Porsche dealership and traded it in for a black Cayenne S. That SUV looked like a beast.

Kim wanted to get a Porsche 911, but I talked her out of it. With two girls and all their shopping trips, that car was too small. She ended up with a white Jaguar Vanden Plas instead, and it fit her perfectly. Not bad for a girl from the hood of Detroit and a country boy from Ohio. We used to laugh about that. It felt like proof that with enough hard work and determination, anything was possible.

Whenever someone from corporate came into town to work with me, I always made a point to introduce them to the best surgeons in the area. When we needed a break, I liked to take them to Paty's in Burbank. It's spelled with one "t," not two. Paty's was a simple lunch spot, but you could always count on good food and a crowd that looked like they belonged in the movies. People sat in booths reading scripts or scribbling on notepads, talking about screenplays.

Sometimes I'd see local doctors there, too. It wasn't fancy, just a comfortable place to eat outside and enjoy the California sun. The studios were only a few blocks away, so you never knew who might be sitting at the next table.

One afternoon, my colleague Craig and I took Dr. Barry Seibel out to lunch in Beverly Hills. Barry was one of the most talented surgeons I knew, sharp and endlessly curious. We went to Kate Mantilini's, a well-known restaurant on Wilshire Boulevard and Doheny. The place had a reputation. It was where people like Mel Brooks, Tony Curtis, Ronald Reagan, and Sammy Davis Jr. used to eat. It opened in the late eighties and quickly became the go-to spot for Beverly Hills business lunches.

Barry loved it so much that he actually took pictures of the bathroom decor because he wanted to redo his at home the same way. Craig and I couldn't stop laughing when he pulled out his phone and started snapping photos inside the restroom. But that was Barry, brilliant, focused, and always paying attention to detail. When he asked you a technical question about an implant or procedure, you'd better remember your answer, because the next time you saw him, he'd ask again.

There were other times when I'd stop in to see my old fraternity brother, Rayford Frye. He owned an optical shop right on Wilshire Boulevard in Beverly Hills. Ray was smooth, always had a good story, and knew everyone worth knowing. Sometimes he'd order Chinese food to the shop, and we'd sit in the loft area eating lunch while people-watching through the big windows that overlooked the boulevard.

Other days, we'd head out back through the alley behind his store that opened onto Bedford Drive. There was a restaurant next door called The Ginger Man. It was owned by Carroll O'Connor, the actor from the old TV show *All in the Family*. Carroll used to have a billboard advertising the place, showing his chef arriving in a Rolls-Royce. I remember hearing that he actually came in sometimes, sitting quietly in a booth in the back, keeping to himself.

Ray and I would sometimes sneak into that same alley between his shop and the restaurant, light up a joint, and then walk inside The Ginger Man to grab a beer and a plate of steamed mussels. Those were simple afternoons that felt like luxury. It wasn't about the food or the cars or even the money. It was the feeling of being alive, of knowing you'd worked hard enough to enjoy the moment and the company around you.

Chapter 12:
Night at the Fight

There were days in Southern California when everything felt like it was moving fast and I was just trying to keep up with it. My work in medical sales had taken off in ways I never could have predicted when I first started. I was calling on big teaching institutions all across Los Angeles. One week I would be at Jules Stein, walking the halls where cutting edge research was happening. The next week I would be over at Doheny Eye Institute, which was affiliated with USC while the other belonged to UCLA. The campuses were different, the energy was different, the politics were different. Yet every visit gave me the same buzz. I felt like I was part of something important. I was helping doctors give people back their most cherished sense. Their sight.

Five years into that career, something major began to happen. The product that had shaped so much of my life, time, energy and belief was called Crystalens. It changed lives every single day and everyone was doing it. Surgeons were proud to be part of the technology. Patients were excited about a new kind of vision that felt unbelievably natural. The company behind it was Eyeonics and Southern California was my territory. Whenever I heard someone mention how many implants were being done, I would feel that jolt of pride inside me. I knew I had played a role. Even if it was small compared to the worldwide numbers, it was still something. Crystallens had already gone into more than ninety five thousand eyes around the globe. That number amazed me then and it still amazes me now.

During that same period, a deal was on the horizon that none of us could ignore. Bausch and Lomb wanted to buy Eyeonics. The whispers began long before anything was announced. People spoke quietly in hallways, pretending they were not curious about what it could mean for them. I listened, I guessed, I hoped, and then one day it became real. The acquisition happened. Suddenly my stock options mattered. I was given fifteen of them at around two dollars a share and they sold for about twelve. That kind of jump made my heart race. It felt like I was finally seeing some payoff from all those miles on the road, those early mornings, those late nights, those patient conversations convincing surgeons to give Crystalens a chance.

Around that same time, I made a decision that would seem crazy to the younger version of me. I gave up my Range Rover for a Porsche Cayenne SUV. I had always liked driving something that felt bold and classy and the Porsche felt like a reward. A little trophy on four wheels. Maybe it was a sign that I was believing in myself a bit more. Maybe it was just a moment where I wanted life to feel a little louder. I do not know. What I do know is that every time I drove it, I felt like I had earned something.

Life at that moment was a whirlwind. Successful days at work. Nice dinners. Sunshine on the freeways. I was seeing all that this career could offer. Then another opportunity came along. Something totally different from ophthalmology or medical sales. Something I had dreamed about since I was young watching boxing legends on TV. I wanted to attend a professional fight. Not just any fight. I wanted to feel the electricity of a big match under the lights.

The chance came when Sugar Shane Mosley was scheduled to fight Ricardo Mayorga at the Home Depot Center. I did not even hesitate. I paid six hundred dollars for a ticket. At the time, that price felt like a huge swing, but I kept thinking that life was meant for these kinds of stories, moments that stick with you long after the money is gone. The night of the fight arrived and I drove up with excitement pounding in my chest.

As soon as I entered the stadium I knew I had stepped into another world. The lights were bright. The music was loud. The air almost tasted like adrenaline. The event had a special parking area for Range Rovers since the brand was sponsoring the fight. I looked around and saw expensive cars everywhere with bodyguards leaning against them like gatekeepers. I laughed a little to myself thinking how crazy it was that my own life had brought me here.

Walking through the crowds, the first thing that hit me was the number of celebrities. Everyone I had ever seen on TV seemed to be walking past me. Then I saw Sylvester Stallone just a little ways away and I almost said his name out loud like a starstruck kid. Don King was also there, his hair shooting skyward like a crown. He was the one promoting the fight and he looked exactly like he did every time he spoke into a microphone about a heavyweight showdown. Jim Lampley was there. Max Kellerman was there. Manny Stewart was part of the HBO announcing team.

All of them were wearing tuxedos and carried themselves like they lived at the very top of this glittering world.

And me. I was sitting only seven rows from the ring.

There was a fighter sitting right in front of me, a Mexican boxer who clearly had fans everywhere. Girls kept rushing up to him for autographs even while punches were flying in the ring. Each time he grabbed a pen they squealed like he was the star of the show. In a way, maybe he was. Then I heard the crowd erupt behind me and when I turned to look, I saw George Lopez standing on his chair, hands raised high as the entire stadium applauded him. He knew how to fire up a crowd without even speaking. He just smiled and let the people adore him.

LaDainian Tomlinson, the running back who owned the NFL at that time, was also there. It almost made me laugh to see so many unbelievably successful people gathered together. I thought to myself, here I am hanging out with the ballers. And it was not lost on me how special that moment really was. It was outdoors too which made everything feel even more alive. The breeze rolled through the stadium and everyone leaned forward, eyes locked on the ring.

The fight itself was unreal. The punches were thrown with a kind of power that could only belong to professionals who lived and breathed that life. When Sugar Shane connected, the sound was like a shotgun in the distance. The crowd jumped to its feet over and over again, everyone screaming, cheering and shouting instructions like the fighters could actually hear us. My heart beat so fast that I felt like I had been in the ring myself. By the end, once Sugar Shane Mosley had defeated Richard Mayorga, I knew this night would go down as one of the most exciting sporting experiences of my life. Nothing could touch it.

Of course, I did not stop there. I loved that rush too much. Later on, I went to another fight and this time I invited my dad to come with me. We had seats on the floor again. Just like before, the crowd was loud and stylish and full of stars. Pop and I looked around at the fancy watches and the giant diamond necklaces. The ladies wore mink coats even though the evenings in Los Angeles were only a little cool. It felt excessive, maybe even ridiculous, but I could also see that the coat on their shoulders was not really about warmth. It was about showing the world that they belonged to a certain kind of life.

Pop and I just enjoyed the show. We laughed and talked and took in every moment. I remember thinking how lucky I was to give him a night like that. We had been through a lot and to sit next to him with the noise and the lights and the thrill of the fight made me grateful in a way I cannot describe, at least not with just a sentence or two.

After one of those fights, I was riding a wave of excitement and I did not want the night to end. So I went over to Magic Johnson's TGI Fridays. It was one of those places that could only happen in Los Angeles. I sat at the bar and ordered a steak and a cocktail and just let myself enjoy the feeling of the entire evening. I looked around and saw people laughing and having late dinners and I thought about how strange it was that my journey through medical sales had led me into restaurants owned by legends and seats next to celebrities at boxing events.

Another perk of my job, maybe one of the best perks, was the number of times I got to take doctors to see the Lakers play. Sometimes it was just one or two doctors and we would get seats near the floor. Other times I teamed up with a couple reps and we would get a luxury box. Those boxes were like tiny VIP apartments built into the arena. We had comfortable seating above the glass with a perfect view of the court. And if you wanted the feel of the action a little closer, you could walk right out and sit in the two rows near the front. The game was always right there for us.

The food inside the box was something out of a dream. It was catered with everything you could imagine. Chicken, beef, pasta, loud trays full of snacks, and drinks ready for anyone who needed another round. At halftime, a woman would knock and then come rolling in with a cart that looked like a moving bakery. Cakes, pies and desserts so pretty that you would almost feel bad eating them. I used to grab something special for Kim and bring it home. Seeing her smile made the whole night feel even better. It was a simple way to share the perks of my job with someone I loved.

For years, those outings were normal in our industry. That was how the business worked. Lunches, dinners, games, golf outings, events. You built relationships through shared experiences. Then everything changed in 2014. Medicare and Medicaid created new rules called The Sunshine Act. They decided that pharmaceutical and medical companies needed strict limits on what they could do for physicians. Suddenly the big entertaining budgets were gone. Expensive office lunches became rare. Fancy dinners became something to avoid. Those boxes at the games, those fights, those golf days, they all became monitored and eventually prohibited. The world of sales became quieter and more controlled. Everyone knew the rules had changed forever.

But back in those days when boxing under the lights was still fair game and perks flowed like confetti, I lived through some unforgettable nights. There were fancy cars surrounding the arena, celebrities blending into crowds, bright lights shining in the Southern California night sky. All of it wrapped itself into a time when it felt like I was moving upward and outward with momentum I had never experienced before.

Those were nights that made me feel alive. Nights when I could look around at a world filled with success and sparkle and think to myself that I had earned a seat in that place. I was working hard. I was pushing forward. And somewhere between the roar of the crowd and the flash of the cameras, I started to believe that anything was possible.

Chapter 13:
Frozen

Growing up as an only child shaped the way I saw people. When you do not have brothers or sisters running down the hallway or fighting over the last biscuit on the dinner table, the cousins and friends you gather along the way become your siblings in spirit. They become your everyday world. They become your shoulders to lean on and the voices cheering you forward when life feels heavy or confusing or bigger than you are ready for. I did not realize it then, but those relationships built the foundation of who I became. Each one left a mark on me. Each one carried a lesson that stayed long after they were gone. Some of them stayed with me through laughter and noise, while others stayed through memory alone because life does not always let us keep the people we love. Sometimes it only lets us hold the echoes of what they gave us.

One of the first of those friends was Deacon Sneed. Everyone called him Deac. I mentioned him briefly before, but he deserves more than just a passing line. When we were teenagers, he was the one who had the car everyone wanted to ride in. You know the kind. The kind of car where the doors never closed quietly and the speakers rattled if you turned the music up too high. The kind of car that gave you freedom when you did not really have any money in your pocket, but all you needed was the right friend behind the wheel. He knew how to get us to concerts and parties and places we probably had no business being, yet somehow it always felt safe.

He had this influence that pulled me forward in a good way. He always spoke life into me. When I was unsure about my future or trying to understand my place in the world, Deac would remind me to stay positive, stay focused, and believe that things would work out. He made me feel like anything I imagined could be real if I worked for it and did not let doubt drown it out. He had that kind of presence. Warm, hopeful, confident.

Cancer took him from this world on a Wednesday in January of 2004. He was only forty-six. I remember hearing the news and feeling winded in a way no punch could ever cause. Losing someone who shaped your early years feels like losing a little piece of youth. It makes you look around and realize time moves whether you are ready or not.

Then there was my cousin Butch. His full name was John Patterson, but Butch was what everyone called him, and it always sounded right to me. He was older, and I saw him the way young boys see superheroes they already know in real life. He had been part of the Black Panther Party when he was young, and although I was too young to fully understand what that meant at the time, I could tell he carried strength and conviction wherever he went. There was a steel confidence in him. At the same time, he had this gentle way of teaching without sounding like he was giving orders.

He could flip me in the backyard like I weighed nothing, and he taught me how to defend myself when I needed to. He graduated from Central State University and later became a lobbyist for a hospital association. I watched him chase his goals with focus. He had a beautiful home in

Columbus and drove a BMW 7 Series that looked like success and sounded like power when the engine rolled to life. I swore to myself I would have a car like that one day. I had no idea it would take years and more work than my young mind could imagine, yet that dream stuck with me.

Butch introduced me to jazz that felt too grown for my young ears. Yet it stuck too. There was something about the horns and the bass lines and the wandering rhythm that felt like lessons I would understand later. And I did. He passed away at sixty-two. When I think of him, I think of jazz on summer evenings, ambition that sets the tone for your life, and a BMW gliding down a smooth street. I think of brotherhood without sharing blood in the traditional sense.

Another memory stands tall in my life. His name was Lawrence Claxton. We both got full scholarships to Western Michigan University in 1977. We were two young men ready to take on the world with track spikes and big dreams. After graduation in 1981, I figured our paths would drift like most college friendships do. Yet life has a funny way of letting some people reappear when you least expect them.

Years later, I walked into The Standard Hotel in downtown Los Angeles, and there he was. Lawrence walked through the door with a group of his Alpha fraternity brothers like a wave of familiar history flooding the room. There was laughter. There were drinks passed around. There was a feeling like time had folded back and given us a few hours from our youth to hold again.

He and another teammate, Warren Miller, came to Los Angeles again years later. I picked them up from their hotel, and we sat together in a restaurant, eating and talking like life had never pushed us into different corners. We shared memories and created new ones. Then, in August 2020, Lawrence passed away. He was only sixty. I still remember that shock and the stillness that followed. That kind of news always seems to pause life for a moment.

Then there was Andre Dawson. We called him Duke. He pledged me in college and later moved to California, just like I had. He had a plan and followed it without hesitation. He became a lieutenant with the Los Angeles Police Department and served the city for 32 years, including investigating human trafficking. That kind of job says something. It says discipline. It says courage. It says heart.

One day, I was driving my old Volvo between the 405 and Marina del Rey when a BMW cut close to me. I hit the brakes and pulled up beside it, ready to speak my mind, then I looked, and there was Duke, smiling like life had just played a trick on us. We pulled over on the freeway shoulder and talked right there while cars rushed by. Nothing extraordinary about the location, yet it felt like a special moment. He passed away at fifty-nine. When I think of him, I remember loyalty and drive.

My cousin Mario was another constant in my young years. We thought we were the Temptations whenever music played in our homes. We practiced steps and sang with conviction, even if we did not always hit the notes. Mario and I moved through childhood like two brothers pulled together by rhythm, imagination, and shared worlds.

His father, my Uncle Ray, was different. He could be strict in a way that left no room for argument. When he told you to be home before the streetlights came on, he meant it like the law. One evening, Mario and I lost track of time. We raced home, thinking we could sneak through the back door without anyone noticing. Uncle Ray sat at the dining table waiting, quiet and calm like a judge who already knew the verdict.

Mario went into the bathroom with him and came out with tears in his eyes. Then Uncle Ray looked at me and simply said, "My mother will handle you." The relief that washed over me in that moment felt like air returning to my lungs.

Uncle Ray worked on cars, and his garage always smelled of oil, grit, and effort. He always said Aunt Jan was his queen, and he kept a little picture of her on a round piece which was about the size of a half-dollar. He had a 57 lime-green Chevy that could tear up pavement if it wanted to. That car was an absolute street beast. On the back, it read "Color Me Gone." The way that car shook the ground when it came to life still lives in my memory.

Years later, when life had grown more complicated and I had a wife and responsibilities, Uncle Ray offered advice that stuck. He reminded my mother that Kim was my wife and that meant something. He stood between tension and helped it settle. He passed from cancer, another life taken before time felt ready.

Mario and I came back close again when we were grown. He worked in the consumer goods business, and one day, we sat outside a store in San Diego, eating lunch on a picnic table with the sun warming our backs. We talked about dreams and about starting a pretzel distributorship. The West Coast had none, and we planned to change that.

We found a warehouse large enough to hold product for three eighteen-wheelers. We planned out our trucks and routes and hired eager people ready to work. Desiree, full of energy and experience, led the charge. Her husband joined later, and our team grew one by one. There was even a guy named Barry who flew in from the East Coast every other week just to take a route and help us.

We supplied Targets, Walmarts, and grocery stores up and down Southern California. It reminded me of my Gallo wine days, only the lift was heavier now, the boxes bigger, the work more physical. Yet it felt good. It felt honest. It felt like building something you could hold in your hands.

One morning, I pulled my truck to the loading dock at a Target in Thousand Oaks. The air was cool. The sun was just waking up over the hills. It felt like another regular day in a busy life. And sometimes that is how life moves. Quiet. Routine. Familiar. Moments blend until one moment changes everything, and the path after that never looks the same.

Late morning light filtered across the valley, and the heat was already rising. It had been a long, hot week, and my shirt stuck to my back as I loaded about ten cases of product onto my hand truck. My routine felt familiar and steady. I checked each box like I had done a thousand times before and then began wheeling the pretzels toward the store entrance. I kept thinking about the day ahead and how much work I still had to do. I planned to get in and out and stay on schedule, just like any other day on the job.

The cool air from inside the store washed over me as I walked through the automatic doors. It felt like relief after being in the sun. I checked in the product with the receiver and did the usual paperwork. It was so routine that my mind barely paid attention. I could probably do it half asleep by now. Once that part was finished, I headed back out with the pretzels and began stocking the shelves. I rolled into the chip aisle, ready to move fast so I could finish this stop and get going.

I started unloading the cases and carrying the product to the right spots on the shelf. Everything felt normal. I lifted boxes and moved down the row. It was nothing unusual. Then my right foot brushed against a case of pretzels. It was only a slight trip, and I steadied myself without giving it much thought. A woman who had been shopping in the aisle looked up at me. She asked if I was okay. I smiled and told her I was fine. It felt like nothing. Just a small stumble. No big deal. I kept working.

Then it happened again. My leg did not feel right. I tried to take another step, and my right leg did not respond.

It was like the message from my brain never made it to my body. I fell again, and this time it shocked me. I told myself I only needed a minute. I thought it was just fatigue, or maybe I moved too quickly. I tried to shake it off, but something was wrong. My leg would not move at all.

I tried again to stand, and suddenly, nothing in my body listened to me. My mind was awake and alert, but from the neck down, I felt like I was trapped. Frozen. I slid backward until my back rested against the shelves full of chips and pretzels. My arm dropped into my lap and stayed limp. My breathing picked up, and fear washed over me. I whispered to myself, asking what was happening to me. My right side felt like it belonged to someone else.

A man walked into the aisle and saw me on the ground. His face changed the moment he looked at me. He hurried over and checked my pulse. Then a woman I had not noticed earlier came toward us from the other direction. I heard her voice, and she sounded calm and steady. She said she was a nurse. She knelt beside me and asked me questions. Before I could answer, a doctor appeared as if it had all been planned in advance. He checked me quickly. It felt unreal to have so many medical professionals in one grocery store aisle at the exact moment I needed them. It was almost like they had been waiting there.

The doctor looked at me and said it sounded like a stroke. He told me to stay still. I told him I could not move if I tried. My voice shook as I explained I felt frozen in my own body. He nodded and spoke to the nurse. She already had her phone out and called for paramedics. Everything felt like it was happening at high speed yet also in slow motion, as if I were watching it from somewhere else.

Within minutes, the paramedics arrived. They came rushing in with equipment and a stretcher. They asked if I could get up. I told them again that I could not move. They lifted me carefully and placed me onto the gurney. The lights above the aisle felt bright and blurry. The ride out of the store felt like a dream that I wanted to wake up from. I glanced back at the shelves and the half-unloaded cases sitting there. It felt strange to leave my work unfinished like that.

The ambulance took me to the hospital in Thousand Oaks. I recognized the place right away. As a sales rep, I had been there before to attend a surgery with a physician who had implanted my lens. The memory flickered through my mind, and it felt like a strange loop in my life. Being a visitor one day and a patient another never crossed my mind before. Life has its own timing, and sometimes it is so unexpected that it makes your head spin.

Tests began almost as soon as they rolled me in. Nurses and doctors moved around me, asking questions and running scans. I could hear machines humming and footsteps echoing in the hallway. They called Kim, and soon she and Shannon arrived. Seeing familiar faces felt like a lifeline. Their voices were gentle yet worried. I could tell they tried to stay calm, but I saw the fear in their eyes. I tried to reassure them, but even speaking was difficult.

That entire weekend passed in the hospital. I could not do anything except wait and trust the people taking care of me. Later, they transferred me to Henry Mayo, which was closer to home. That made things easier for the family to visit. Sydney and Kim came to see me there. Their presence gave me strength even though I could barely move. I stayed there for about a month before going to rehab. Time moved slowly in that place. Each day felt long, but every small improvement felt like a victory.

There was a doctor named Dr Terrazino who often came in during the evenings. He checked on me and talked to me like a friend, not just a patient. That mattered more than he probably realized. After a while, they finally discharged me, and I went home. I remember the first day I tried to transfer from my chair to the bed. That simple movement felt like climbing a mountain. I practiced over and over, and it exhausted me, but I was determined to learn.

One moment stands out. I came home and rolled behind the chair. I did not lock the wheels, and Kim helped me sit. The chair rolled backward, and both of us went down to the floor. We looked at each other with surprise, and then we laughed. We were lying there face to face, and all I could say was that I forgot to lock the wheels. It was one of those moments that could have been frustrating but turned into a memory I cherish. Because in that moment, we were not defeated. We just laughed and tried again.

Recovery continued with Rehab Without Walls. A team of therapists came regularly to work with me. They pushed me and encouraged me. They celebrated every small milestone with me. First, I learned to shower by myself. Then I could take care of basic needs. Later, I walked with a walker and then a cane. Each step gave me hope. Simple things like standing to cook became possible again, even though Kim still prepared most meals and made sure I ate right. She watched my vitals and made sure everything was safe. She stayed on top of every detail. She has always had my back. Even today, she keeps an eye on me, and I am grateful for that love and loyalty.

I think back to our college years when she would bring me sandwiches from the cafeteria. She always took care of me then, and she still does now. Forty-plus years of marriage, and nothing has changed in that way. I thank God for blessing me with her. Some people talk about loyalty, but she lives it every single day. She is my ride or die girl and always has been.

Friends reached out too. Greg Kimball and Jay Jackson came by to check on me. Their visits reminded me that brotherhood does not fade. Those bonds hold steady through time, no matter where life takes us. Then one day, I got a call from my aunt Jan. She told me Mario had passed. He had a heart attack. My chest felt heavy hearing the news. I called his son, and he cried so hard that neither of us could say much. I still cry over Mario. He passed on October 22nd, 2022. It was almost one month after I got out of the hospital. The loss felt sharp and sudden.

Later, I tried calling Jay. I left messages, but there was no answer. Something did not feel right. I sat at my computer and searched for him. I looked up the Boys and Girls Club in Burbank, where he worked. They had a website with staff photos and departments. I scrolled through, and then I saw his picture. Under it, the comments said RIP. The moment my eyes focused on those letters, my heart dropped. I yelled out in shock. Kim came rushing downstairs, asking what had happened. I sat there sobbing. I searched again and found his obituary. He passed on July 30th, 2024, from complications after surgery while recovering from prostate cancer. He was seventy-two, but he looked like he was forty-two. Strong. Healthy. Full of energy. I never expected to find his name that way.

Life has a way of surprising you. One moment you are unloading pretzels in a grocery aisle, and the next you are lying on the floor unable to move. One moment you laugh with a friend, and later you discover they are gone. It all reminds you that time is precious and uncertain. Recovery became not only physical but emotional, too. Every memory came with weight and meaning.

I keep moving forward. I keep working on strength and mobility. I wake up grateful for another chance to stand, walk, and live life with the people I love. I think about the faces that were there in the most unexpected moment in that aisle and how strangers became angels that day. I think about the friends I miss and the ones still beside me. I take each day one step at a time, just like those first steps with the walker. I breathe. I remember. And I keep going without knowing what tomorrow will bring.

Reflections

When I look back, growing up in Yellow Springs, despite being in a rather redneck state, that little town was a great place. It was very diverse, full of interesting and actually smart people. I was glad to have grown up there. I developed some great relationships, and while I did not have many, I had some very good friends who were more like brothers than anything else. While I was not the smartest kid in school, I was hungry to succeed in something, not really knowing what, but I knew I wanted to have a good job, perhaps get married, raise a family, and be successful in whatever I did. I was told that if I learned a trade, I could possibly be a success. Would that be it for me? And I wanted to go to college, not really sure where, but I knew that I wanted to go.

And wouldn't you know it, I ended up going to Western Michigan University on a full ride with a track scholarship. When I went, I was not really sure what I was going to major in. I just knew graduating could possibly guarantee me something, and what that was, I had no idea. I was never a big consumer of alcohol, though drinking in college kind of goes with the territory. I did smoke a fair amount of weed, but so did a lot of college athletes, and many still do today.

The one thing I did, though, was dream. I would sit around with my frat brother and roommate and figure out what was going on, what would happen after graduation, and where I would go. This would be a step-by-step process, and college was a place where you find yourself. For me, it was California. I thought about customer-service-type jobs to start. When you see things, you say to yourself, Hey, I would not mind doing that. I saw salespeople coming in and out of that student store at UCLA.

Before you know it, I ended up in the pharmaceutical business. Then what happens is you go to the meetings and you see other people walk across that stage for being one of the best, and I felt that same feeling. It was not just enough to be working for a pharmaceutical medical sales company. I wanted that recognition. But now I had to use my brain versus my brawn. Living in Los Angeles, you can get caught up in things, too. You see things you want, you see things you desire. I stepped out of line one time. I almost cheated on Kim. Physically, it never happened. She kept me in line.

In sales, I traveled all over the place. I learned how to educate eye surgeons and made good money doing it. And just like track, I received awards and recognition for my accomplishments. This is surely not a template for any young person, for we all choose different paths. As for me, I survived both a stroke and prostate cancer. I see all my brothers and friends who have passed away, and I always ask myself, *Why did the Lord not take me?*

I remember when I used to travel. I flew a lot, and there have been times when the flight was bumpy, and I used to pray to myself, asking, "God, please do not let me die now. I have got more I want to do." Well, I have been able to walk with the help of my trustworthy cane, and though I have no use in my right arm, I feel blessed. I am happy when

I get up in the morning and watch the morning sun come up. I feel satisfied I did a lot, so when it is time for me to go, I can simply say, "Thank you, Lord."

1 Corinthians 9:24-27

Do you not know that in a race all the runners run, yet only one receives the prize? So run that you may obtain it. Every athlete exercises self-control in all things. They do it to receive a perishable wreath, but we do it to receive an imperishable one. So I do not run aimlessly. I do not box as one beating the air. But I discipline my body and keep it under control, lest after preaching to others I myself should be disqualified.

2 Timothy 4:7

I have fought the good fight, I have finished the race, I have kept the faith.

Peace.

www.ingramcontent.com/pod-product-compliance
Lightning Source LLC
Chambersburg PA
CBHW071155300726
48975CB00004B/1171